His fingertips against her scalp pressed harder, bringing her even closer to him. Their bodies brushed and Gracie forgot all about the cold and the people after them. She could only think about his mouth, right there, so close, and somehow he was doing this. Pushing this.

And he wasn't running away.

"I've needed you this whole time," he said, and his lips were so close to hers she could practically feel the words against her mouth. "I don't know anything about being a good man. I know less about moving forward or new lives or living period. Not anymore."

"I could teach you," she whispered, moving onto her toes so she could be that much closer to what she wanted. A new life. Moving forward. It might be the completely wrong time, but how could she not take what she wanted when it was right here? She knew how precarious it all was.

"I think you could," he murmured, and then he closed that last distance, his mouth finally, finally meeting hers.

WYOMING CHRISTMAS RANSOM

———

NICOLE HELM

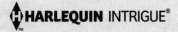

HARLEQUIN INTRIGUE®

To my husband, who also almost always answers my questions with "That wouldn't happen," but indulges me when I say "But *could* it happen?"

ISBN-13: 978-1-335-52681-6

Wyoming Christmas Ransom

Copyright © 2018 by Nicole Helm

Recycling programs for this product may not exist in your area.

Printed in U.S.A.

HARLEQUIN®
www.Harlequin.com

Nicole Helm grew up with her nose in a book and the dream of one day becoming a writer. Luckily, after a few failed career choices, she gets to follow that dream—writing down-to-earth contemporary romance and romantic suspense. From farmers to cowboys, Midwest to *the* West, Nicole writes stories about people finding themselves and finding love in the process. She lives in Missouri with her husband and two sons and dreams of someday owning a barn.

Books by Nicole Helm

Harlequin Intrigue

Carsons & Delaneys

Wyoming Cowboy Justice
Wyoming Cowboy Protection
Wyoming Christmas Ransom

Stone Cold Texas Ranger
Stone Cold Undercover Agent
Stone Cold Christmas Ranger

Harlequin Superromance

A Farmers' Market Story

All I Have
All I Am

Falling for the New Guy
Too Friendly to Date
Too Close to Resist

Visit the Author Profile page at Harlequin.com.

CAST OF CHARACTERS

Gracie Delaney—Bent County's coroner, she's been helping Will Cooper investigate his wife's car accident for two years. Worried about Will's mental state, she's ready to stop helping him.

Will Cooper—Something of a hermit since his wife's cheating was discovered through her death. Will has spent the past two years trying to prove his late wife's death wasn't an accident.

Paula Cooper—Will's late wife, who died in a car crash, which was ruled an accident.

Laurel Delaney—Gracie's cousin and a sheriff's deputy who steps in to help investigate the case when Will's car is tampered with.

Cam, Jen and Dylan Delaney—Gracie's cousins, who work together to help keep her safe.

Ty and Noah Carson—Distant relations of Paula Cooper, but agree to help Gracie and Will try to figure out who Paula had been having an affair with.

Jesse Carson—Paula's uncle who hates the Delaneys.

Geoff Delaney—Gracie's uncle (Laurel, Cam, Dylan and Jen's father) who raised Gracie after her parents died when she was a child.

Chapter One

Gracie Delaney didn't care for the nickname "Angel of Death," but in Bent, Wyoming, it was something of the truth. If she came to a person's door unannounced, they knew what was coming.

The fact that she was young, maybe a little girl-next-door looking, no longer fooled people. As the coroner for Bent County, Gracie's work was death.

It wasn't as bad as some people made it out to be. Considering her parents had died in a car crash when she'd been six, and she was the lone survivor of said crash, she'd been intimately acquainted with death her whole life.

Funny, life was a lot harder than death. Death was easy, and it was final. The cause might occasionally be a mystery, but it was a mystery she always solved.

Gracie blew out a breath as she parked her car in Will Cooper's yard. Life, meanwhile, had a hundred mysteries she couldn't figure out. Like why two years after she'd informed Will Cooper of his wife's death, she still came to check in on him routinely.

She'd informed a lot of people of their loved ones' deaths over the course of two years, and while some reactions stuck with her, maybe a few even haunted her, only Will's reaction had ever caused her to act outside a professional capacity.

She supposed it was the fact he couldn't accept his wife had simply skidded off the road and crashed into a tree. He insisted the detectives had missed or overlooked things. He'd become obsessed with proving foul play.

Gracie had felt sorry for him and his inability to accept the truth. So, she'd let him have access to records she shouldn't have let him have access to. She'd shown him, over and over again, how the only thing that had killed his wife was an icy road and a tree.

Still he pushed into this theory that whoever his wife had been having an affair with had been the one to kill her.

Gracie got out of the truck and stared at the ramshackle cabin Will currently lived in. He still owned the pretty little two-story he and his wife had shared in Bent proper, but rented it out to a family with kids. He claimed it was because up here he could do his metalwork without any neighbor complaint, but Gracie figured it was something more isolating than all that.

He wasn't a Bent native. He'd moved here after marrying Paula Carson and though he'd lived in town and been building a name for himself with his metalwork, Paula's death had changed him. He'd isolated himself and since he had no family in Bent, no natives had been too worried about a stranger's hermit behavior.

Except Gracie. For all intents and purposes, she was his only link to the outside world.

God, she wished she could help him.

"You're going to," she said to herself. "Right here. Right now." She'd been playing into his obsession for too long, and it had to stop. No more looks at old reports. No more trips to that road to study curves and angles. She'd still be his friend, but that was it. Like a drug dealer refusing to continue to deal an addict their drug of choice.

Will was going to have to go cold turkey or solo. Her chest tightened and for the briefest second she considered retracing her steps. He'd go solo. She knew he would, and she didn't want him to.

She wanted to fix him. To help him. And yes, maybe she was a little inappropriately hung up on the guy, but that only factored into it a little.

She shook that thought away and started for the cabin. No Christmas lights, not a hint that it was December and even rough-and-tumble Bent had brought out its Christmas decor. But not for Will. She wasn't certain he celebrated anything anymore.

She heard the faint strains of music and bypassed the cabin door, instead walking around the cabin to the back. He had the doors open on his shed, and inside he worked on a metal project.

He'd once had a blacksmith shop down in town, something both local ranchers had used and tourists had gotten a kick out of. But he'd closed it after Paula's death. In fact, he hadn't worked for a year after, living off the rent from the house.

Slowly over the past year he'd gotten back into metalwork. Little artistic projects he made custom for ranches, or occasionally sold to the antique store in town.

Gracie had been hopeful it was a sign he'd give up obsessing over the mystery of Paula's affair and death. Like so many times with him, her hopes had been dashed.

And you are done being a silly, too-hopeful girl.

She nodded to herself as she crossed the yard. He worked, mask over his face, black T-shirt clinging to his chest even with the cold air around them. He was working with some tool that shot a flame out of it in one hand, clamps in another as he heated and twisted metal. Faint lines of grime and sweat streaked across his impressive forearms and his biceps strained against the sleeves of his T-shirt.

She allowed herself a dreamy sigh, because he wouldn't hear her over the noise of the tools. Because this was it. She was cutting ties. Well, she was cutting off the supply of information. She just had a sinking suspicion that meant he'd cut ties with her, too.

He turned off the blowtorch thing, nudging the mask up on his head to reveal his face. A few trickles of sweat dripped down his square jaw, and she didn't know why she found that appealing.

"Hey," he offered. "You bring those pictures?"

Gracie shook her head. "No, Will. I didn't."

He frowned, setting down the tools and pulling the mask completely off his face. "Then why are you here?"

Ouch. She forced herself to smile. "I always come hang out on Friday afternoons."

"Usually with the thing I asked you for, though."

"I'm not..." She cleared her throat. "I can't keep bringing you stuff."

He frowned, eyebrows drawing together as he stared at her. Not just anger, but confusion, as if it didn't make any sense to him.

How could it not make sense? "For two years I've helped you try to undermine both my investigation and the police's. I'm..." She swallowed at the nerves flapping around in her chest and throat. "I'm done," she said, wishing it had come out more forcefully and not so wobbly.

"Done," he said flatly.

"I'm still your frie—"

"I don't need a friend. I never did."

Ouch. Ouch. Ouch. "Okay." She wouldn't cry in front of him. She couldn't allow herself to show the hurt. It was so stupid. She'd all but forced her company on him for two years. He might be the obsessive one, but she was pathetic.

She turned, blinking back the tears that burned in her eyes as she forced her lead-like legs to move back toward her car.

"Where are you going?" he called after her.

"Home," she said, hoping he couldn't read that squeak in her voice. Oh, who was she kidding? He didn't care. If it didn't have to do with the case, he did not care. She'd been a means to an end, and she couldn't be anymore.

"Why?"

She laughed, surprised at the way bitterness could grow just as large as sadness. "You don't want a friend, and I can't keep being your supplier. So." What else was there to say?

Apparently nothing, because Will didn't try to stop her after that. She got to her truck, didn't bother to look back and drove away.

It was time she moved on. Not just for Will, but for herself.

Will watched Gracie get into her truck. He had no idea what had just happened. And damn if it wasn't at the worst possible time.

After two years of combing through everything, he'd found a secret file on Paula's computer within an old grocery list. It didn't name the man she'd had an affair with, but it gave some clues. Will thought maybe a few pictures of the accident might unearth a clue that was connected.

Of course, he had those pictures memorized at this point. He had everything memorized. Losing Gracie's help didn't really matter one way or another. Though it was nice to have someone to bounce ideas off of.

Nice to have someone who didn't look at him like he was crazy, especially on days when he thought he *was* a little crazy. After all, what man investigated the death of his cheating wife for two years? Especially after every law enforcement agency involved had found no reason to believe foul play was involved.

But he felt it. Knew it. Maybe his marriage had been a mess, but that didn't mean he could just *let it go*. Someone had murdered her, he was sure of it. They had to be brought to justice.

Justice would bring him peace. He was sure of that, too.

Regardless of whether or not it was crazy, this

was the man he was. Had been for two years, so it didn't make sense Gracie was quitting out of the blue.

Will cleaned up his tools, frowning at the custom order he was making. It wasn't turning out how he would have liked. He was going to have to start over, but right now wasn't the time. He had to work through this thing with Gracie first or his concentration would be shot.

Something had to have happened. Maybe a friend or family member had warned her off him? Gracie was part of the Delaneys, all law enforcement and politicians and upstanding citizens.

Paula, who'd grown up in the Carson clan, had always said that—*upstanding citizens*—with such disdain because Carsons and Delaneys didn't seem to have much between them besides disdain and bitterness.

Will hadn't much cared one way or another about the silly feud so many Bent citizens held such stock in. Land disputes and romantic tragedies that happened over a century ago didn't really interest him, but he'd sided with the Carsons if asked out of loyalty to Paula.

But Paula was dead, and he wasn't building any monuments in her honor. Their marriage and relationship had gone sour before her untimely death.

He hated to think that was what drove him—the tangle of screwed-up emotions that came with losing someone you'd once loved and then had grown to hate.

He shook his head. It wasn't *that*. It was that he knew something was wrong. For starters, Paula had been on the road to *his* cabin, a place she never went to even when their marriage hadn't basically been over. She hadn't had her purse, and she hadn't been wearing shoes. Which was the opposite of the nearly anal woman he'd been married to for five years.

Now she'd been gone two, and whoever her lover had been was a mystery no one seemed to care to solve.

Except him. Occasionally Gracie suggested it was some warped sense of pride, needing to know the man his wife had chosen over him, more than it was his concern over her death being wrongful.

Wouldn't that make this easier?

He just knew Paula too well for her wreck to make sense, and he couldn't live with himself thinking there might be a murderer out there.

It was likely more emotionally complicated than that, but he chose to focus on the case, on the facts, over those messy emotions that plagued him from where he'd shoved them deep down.

He frowned over at where Gracie's truck had been parked, trying to go through the whole interaction. He'd been a little curt with her, but she knew how he could get when a project wasn't going the way he wanted.

The truth was, Gracie was about the only human contact he had on a regular basis these days, and he'd gotten to taking for granted that it would always continue.

She had to be bluffing. She'd be back tomorrow morning with coffee, an apology and those pictures.

He was sure of it. Certain.

Except the next morning came and went, and so did the next, and by the time an entire week had passed without one peep from Gracie, Will was downright pissed. Where did she get off just cutting him off like that? Abandoning him just like...

He grimaced at that thought as he studied the keys hanging from the hook in his kitchen. He needed food and supplies. Usually Gracie brought him everything he needed so he had to go into town only once a month.

Or less.

Truth be told, everything in his life had narrowed, incrementally, over the past two years. Without Gracie to take his mind off it, this past week had been a glaring reminder.

He didn't like to leave his little mountain. He didn't like to drive. He didn't like to face Bent with its people who knew him and his story. Poor widower. The man who couldn't let the past go.

He didn't trust that world out there, but if he didn't get over it, he was going to starve. He grabbed the keys and started for his door.

But about halfway through he turned around and headed for his—well, Paula's—computer. He could stand to go over the secret file one more time.

He pulled up the document he'd found after meticulously going through every file in her computer, no matter how innocuous the title. This particular file was listed as Grocery List 5/16.

The first page was even a list of groceries. He'd bypassed it he didn't know how many times over the years because it was clearly a grocery list even after a few scrolls. Then he'd decided to not just skim through every file, but to read through every word in case some clue was hidden in the midst of some article about tax law or a random to-do list.

He hadn't found it in any of her files from her job as a CPA, but he had found something in this grocery list. He'd noticed just last week that the list repeated itself after ten vegetables. Which was weird. Why would a grocery list need to repeat itself?

So he'd scrolled. For ten pages. Just the same ten vegetables repeated, and then there was what he'd been looking for.

They appeared to be emails with the to/from stripped out of them, but Paula had kept the dates and the subject lines. Love letters. Well, more like sex letters if Will was honest with himself.

It had been hard to read them, knowing his wife had received them while they were still trying to work things out. Sickening really, but he'd needed a clue.

He *still* needed a clue. So he read them again, sick to his stomach and angry all over again. But he did it. Focusing on every detail, every word choice, every mention of meeting.

He jotted down the referenced meetings this time, then cross-referenced with the computer calendar based on the dates of the email.

And that was when he found his pattern.

Chapter Two

Gracie plastered a smile on her face as the party around her was hitting full swing.

Usually a Delaney wouldn't be caught dead in Rightful Claim, a Carson bar, but the whole town had made an exception to the normal way of town feud bitterness with the engagement party of Gracie's cousin Laurel to the bar's proprietor, Grady Carson.

Gracie was happy for Laurel, probably happier than most of the other Delaneys, who thought the Carsons were a vortex of evil, but the happy couldn't smother her self-absorbed worry over Will.

She hated that she was worried about him when he clearly saw her as nothing, but she didn't think he'd come off his little mountain, and he had to be running low on food.

It's none of your business if he starves to death. That's his own problem.

She wanted to believe that, but whether he cared

back or not, Gracie did care about Will. Even if it was one-sided. Even if it was stupid or pathetic, she cared about him.

Gracie made a beeline for the bar. She usually didn't drink, didn't like the way it made her feel a little dizzy, a little out of control, but maybe it would shush some of this endless circling her brain was doing.

It's not your brain. It's your heart.

Yeah, she really needed to shut that voice up, but before she made it to the crowded bar, she glanced at the door as it opened.

Will stepped in. Underneath a cheerful swath of Christmas lights that looked out of place in this rough-and-tumble, Wild West–themed bar, but also somehow perfect.

For a second she figured she was seeing things she wanted to see, and berated herself for being an idiot. But Will was striding through the room, ignoring any looks or comments, and heading straight for her.

She could only stare for a moment. Will rarely came into town, and when he did it was only to the general store, the gas station or the post office. And he never went anywhere when there might be a crowd.

"Will, what are you—"

"I found something out," he said resolutely. "I need your help."

Gracie glanced around the bar. More than a few pairs of eyes were on them. She knew what they all thought, too. Will Cooper was crazy, and silly Gracie Delaney placated him because she didn't know any better.

Well, she'd figured out how to know better, but she didn't need to prove it to the group.

"Let's talk outside," she whispered, not wanting to draw more attention. She hesitated a second, then brazened through. She linked her arm with his as if they were friends, or more, and headed for the door.

Will came easily, and if she wasn't totally imagining things, a tremor went through his arm, maybe his whole body.

She didn't want to feel sorry for him, or be drawn into whatever help he needed, but surely it was important if Will was facing Bent and Rightful Claim and a party.

He pulled his arm from hers after they pushed through the swinging front doors of Rightful Claim. He took a few steps down the boardwalk, raking his hands through his hair, which needed a trim. Even in the warm glow of the town's twinkle-light-wrapped streetlights, he somehow looked a little wilder, a little more desperate than the last time she'd seen him.

Or that's what you want, idiot.

"I didn't know Rightful Claim got so busy," he

offered, and though the sounds of the party drifted out into the cold night, it was mostly quiet out here.

"It's a party. Laurel and Grady's engagement party."

"Oh. Guess that explains your truck being here." He blew out a breath, looking away from the bar and out at the night sky, which was a sparkling, vast thing. "It's December," he said, as if he hadn't known.

"Yes. Hence the Christmas decorations."

He looked around. Tinsel-lined candy canes Gracie suspected had been around since before she was born hung off the streetlight poles just as they had when she'd been a kid.

"I'm sorry I'm interrupting. It's just I found something."

"Will—" She couldn't do this. For herself as much as for him.

"I found a pattern, to how they met. Wednesdays. Always at six. I don't know where, but there has to be something there. Wednesdays." His gaze fixed on hers in the cheerful Christmas lights.

She'd told him she was done, but here he was, stepping outside his comfort zone and marching into the bar. She was torn between pleasant surprise that he'd braved some of the things he'd been avoiding more and more and being annoyed he thought he could just waltz into her life and demand help.

"Then what?" she asked softly. Because this was what had brought her to that moment last week when she'd cut him off. When she'd cut herself off. She could keep giving him pictures and files and peeks at evidence and what have you, but *then what*? It was an endless circle, and she couldn't be a part of it anymore.

She wanted him to break free of it, too, but she had no say over him. She only had say over herself. But maybe… Maybe if he actually stopped to think about the question like she'd had to…

"What happens if we follow the pattern?" she prodded.

"We follow the clues and—"

"Then what after that? You find the guy your wife was cheating with? You question him and maybe he even had something to do with it despite all evidence to the contrary. The searching is over, you have your answers, your justice. What then?" Because she'd been foolishly hoping to help him to that *what then*, but she had a terrible feeling she'd spent the past two years only aiding him in becoming more screwed up, more of a hermit and less of the easy-going Will Cooper she'd known peripherally before Paula's death.

And because she cared about him, but had zero actual responsibility or hold on him, she had to walk away.

"We'll have the truth," Will said, as if *she* was the

one living in a fantasy world. "I've been searching for the truth for two years. I don't know why you're giving up, but I can't. I can't ignore two years' worth of something telling me this is all wrong."

"What will you do with whatever truth you're after?"

He looked at her a bit like she'd struck him. "Hopefully put a murderer in jail." He shook his head. "Why? Why are you doing this? After all this time, you're just abandoning me. I don't get it."

He actually sounded and looked hurt, instead of just irritated he didn't have help anymore, so she gave him the truth. "I care about you, Will, and I can't keep watching you get worse."

WILL COULDN'T PROCESS those words, or the soft look in Gracie's brown eyes. *Care.* Such a weird word. Such a dangerous thing, to care about someone. You couldn't control what they'd do with that. Couldn't predict it. You could feel safe and happy one minute, eviscerated and broken the next.

Care. No. It gave him a full-body chill. "Get worse at what?" he asked, working to pretend the first part of that sentence didn't exist.

She blew out a breath, lights from the tacky Christmas decorations all around creating a sort of warm yellow glow around her. Occasionally, the few nights he managed to sleep well enough to dream, he'd dream of her, much like this. Something like an angel, down to the glowing.

He wasn't fanciful enough to believe in things like angels, but he wasn't so cynical he couldn't believe that Gracie was part of his life for a reason.

So why was she leaving it?

She blew out a breath. "You said you don't need a friend, but I'm always here if you decide you do. But I'm done playing detective. It was an accident, Will. An *accident*."

"She was not cheating on me accidentally."

"No."

"What changed? Something did, because a person doesn't just walk away after…" It all lodged a little too hard, the words he was saying, a very painful realization he'd come here for the very, very stupid reason of feeling abandoned, and that overly sympathetic look on her face.

He tried to say he had to leave, but he wasn't sure any words actually came out of his mouth. He was moving too fast away from her and this town and…

This was why he stayed up there. When he came down to town, when people were around, talking about things not related to Paula's death, all these messy, confusing, complicated and mixed-up emotions boiled up and over. Who wanted to live in the center of all those things? He didn't understand these people walking through life like it wasn't a relentless parade of suck.

He didn't need Gracie to be his friend. He didn't need anyone to be his friend. He most certainly didn't need fake Christmas crap surrounding him to the point of suffocation.

Who cared if Gracie had a reason for backing out? It wasn't the same as learning your wife was cheating on you, or that she was dead. None of this was the *same*.

But somewhere in the past few years he'd lost how to parse it all. Which meant he'd let this all go—Gracie, her help, anything to do with Bent. He'd figure this all out on his own where he was safe from the way people were complicated, from the way people could betray you.

"Will. Wait."

But he couldn't wait. He had to get back to his house, his mountain. Far away from all *this*.

He turned away from her, hunching against the cold. There were cars everywhere, filling the lot, clogging both sides of the street. He'd had to park two blocks down.

Before turning the corner to where his Jeep was parked, he gave a final glimpse at Gracie standing there in the twinkling lights, hugging herself and looking worried and like a Christmas gift.

He damn well didn't need her worry. Or care.

He climbed into his Jeep and started the engine. He drove out of Bent, so distracted with the roiling set of emotions inside him it took miles to realize something wasn't right.

The engine was making a horrible noise, and the steering wheel wasn't responding the way it normally did. Will frowned. It was pitch-black on this mountain road and not a good place to stop. Even though traffic wasn't a big concern, 18-wheelers sometimes rumbled by toward Fairmont.

If he stopped—

The thought, the hope he could fix this situation, died in an instant. When his foot tapped the brake, nothing happened. He swallowed at the trickle of fear, pressing his foot down harder. A grinding noise sounded—a terrible one—and the brake barely responded, slowing his progress only a little bit.

Will swore as he continued to stomp his foot on the brake. Horrible noise, a slight decrease in speed, but not enough. Keeping his eyes on the road and one hand gripped to the steering wheel for dear life, he fished his phone out from the messy console.

He waited for a straightaway on the road, searched for anything that might slow his car down without killing him. All there was in the dark night, he knew, were rocks and trees and death. He couldn't even see the moon, like some kind of terrible omen.

He dialed Gracie's number, impatiently swearing

as it rang over and over again. He remembered the emergency brake, stomped on the lever, but nothing happened.

She didn't answer.

Stupid to call her instead of 911, and still he gripped his phone with one hand, while desperately trying to take the curves of the dark road ahead of him. Screeching tires, increasing speed as the road dipped, entire car shuddering.

"Gracie," he shouted into his phone when her voice mail beep sounded. "I need your help."

But he couldn't explain beyond that because he had to drop the phone to grip the steering wheel with both hands. Except that didn't seem to help. His steering had gone the way of the brakes and now he was careening toward another curve, this time with no hope of doing anything but catapulting over the edge and into a grove of trees.

Paula's trees.

Chapter Three

Gracie chewed her lip as she stared at her phone. Maybe Will had been calling to apologize. Maybe she should have answered.

He was dealing with such complicated emotions and—

Well, no, the problem was he *had* complex emotions, grief and betrayal, and for two years he'd run away and hermited away from them rather than face them, deal with them, accept them.

And she'd placated and enabled him at every turn. She chewed harder on her lip, staring at the voice mail icon.

"Here. Turn that frown upside down."

Gracie looked up at Laurel, who had slid a bottle of beer in front of her at her little corner table where she was sitting. By herself.

"Sorry I'm not reveling."

"Don't worry. The Carsons are doing enough reveling for all of us," Laurel said, smiling fondly at the motley crew around them. Delaneys lined the outskirts of the crowd. Most looking a little sour faced, though a few had imbibed enough to mingle with Carsons.

Gracie looked back down at her phone. She should put it away and celebrate her cousin's engagement. Celebrate the fact the town wasn't imploding over a Carson and a Delaney getting married.

Yet.

"What's up, Gracie? It isn't like you to mope."

Gracie shook her head, gesturing at the crowd. "It's so not important. I'll tell you about it later. Enjoy your night."

Laurel took a sip from her bottle of beer then glanced around the room, her smile going soft when it landed on her fiancé, Grady Carson. He was laughing with his cousins Noah and Ty behind the bar. They made a handsome, dangerous trio.

Gracie glanced down at her phone again, that obnoxious voice mail icon staring at her.

"So, who's the guy?"

Gracie's head jerked to Laurel. "What?"

"I know everyone you know, Gracie," Laurel said with a smile. "They're all here. So the only reason you're staring at your phone and not talking to anyone is…well, a guy."

Gracie tried to laugh casually, but it came out

sounding forced even to her own ears. "There's no guy."

"Then what's with the phone staring?"

"I'm in a deadly battle of *Candy Crush*."

Laurel laughed. "Liar."

"It's not a guy...per se. I just finally told Will I'd stop..." Gracie shook her head. "This is not engagement party talk."

Laurel reached across the table and patted Gracie's arm. Laurel had never been shy about her disapproval of Gracie's odd relationship with Will. As a sheriff's deputy, Laurel didn't take kindly to accusations that the department wasn't doing its best because the victim had been a Carson, or any of Will's other accusations over the case.

So, it made Gracie feel silly and small bringing it up, especially at Laurel's party.

"He's not my favorite person, but I know you felt a kind of obligation to him, and cutting that off couldn't have been easy."

Gracie forced herself to smile. "And something we can discuss tomorrow."

Laurel nodded. "Fair enough. Just one little piece of advice. Either cut all of it off for good, or accept you're going to be a part of it. Don't sit here in a back-and-forth. Make a choice and stick with it. You'll feel a lot better."

"Aren't you going to tell me which choice?"

"You two look far too serious for a party," Grady said, coming up to them and taking Laurel's hand in his. "On your feet. You're going to dance with me."

"I'm a terrible dancer," Laurel returned with a laugh, but she let Grady pull her to her feet. She left her beer bottle, grinning as Grady gave her a little spin toward the small throng of people dancing to "Rockin' Around the Christmas Tree."

But Laurel smiled over her shoulder at Gracie. "You pick the one you can live with," she called over the crowd and the music.

One she could live with. Gracie frowned. That was the worst advice she'd ever been given. She couldn't live with *either* possibility. She had told him she couldn't help him anymore because she was afraid she was making him worse. She meant that choice, but it didn't make it easy.

She cared about Will. Had even said it to his face and watched him blanch outside this very bar. As if care was some kind of horrible disease she'd foisted upon him.

You decided to cut him off, so cut him off.

She nodded, willing herself to hit the voice mail button, which she did. Then willing herself to hit Delete without listening to a second. For that act, she paused.

She'd cut him off. He didn't want a friend. He was allergic to emotion and she was no therapist, so she couldn't possibly fix him. She couldn't go after him and make things right because he was too closed off, too obsessed, too...

She hit Play, then berated herself. She wasn't going to listen. She was *not* going to listen or get dragged into helping him with things that weren't any good for him.

"Gracie."

Oh hell, she had to listen.

"I need your help." Said in a breathless, gritty voice, as if he was straining against something. Some horrible screeching noise went on in the background, so loud she could barely hear his voice over it.

"Laurel," she yelled, already on her feet, already heading for the door. "Who's on duty at county?"

WILL THOUGHT HE heard sirens. Which was weird. He couldn't hear sirens in his cabin. He couldn't hear anything except bird song, and the occasional rumble of an engine on Fridays.

Gracie. Always Gracie.

It registered, vague and faint, somewhere in the recesses of his brain, that he was cold. And uncomfortable.

No, not uncomfortable, on fire. Painful fire, frigid cold. It didn't make any sense and he couldn't seem to open his eyes.

Well, this was bad.

Something like panic fluttered in his chest, but everything in his body was throbbing with pain. He wasn't at home in his cabin. He wasn't on his mountain. He was somewhere… Somewhere.

He couldn't open his eyes, and he couldn't move without a fiery agony spreading through his body. Things were digging into him and one arm was at an uncomfortable angle tangled up in something hard.

He could still hear sirens, but it was all so far off he wondered if it had anything to do with him or if it was just all in his head.

Then they stopped. Just stopped.

He was going to die, wasn't he? Something had gone wrong with his car. He didn't quite remember what, but everything had gone wrong and he'd crashed and he was going to die.

Just like Paula. Exactly like it.

"Will? Will!"

He must be hallucinating. There'd be no reason Gracie would be out this way. Certainly no reason she'd be his saving grace. Gracie. Grace. He might have laughed if he didn't think his head would roll right off.

"Will? Oh my— I found him!" she shouted, and he could almost hear her or someone or something next to his ear.

"Will. Oh God. Will. Please." When she touched him he groaned, because everything hurt, even Gracie's very welcome touch.

"You're alive. You're alive." She whispered it over and over, her hand still on his chest. He felt the gentle brush of her fingertips across his forehead. Finally a part of his body that didn't hurt.

"Say something, Will. If you're awake. If you can hear me. Say something. Please."

He heard footsteps and a murmur of someone else, but Gracie was talking to him and her fingers were on his face. She sounded desperate and afraid, and he didn't want that for her. No.

He tried to open his eyes again, and this time they went a little. Everything was dark though there was some kind of light, but he couldn't see right. He could tell that. Nothing was right.

His Jeep had malfunctioned. He'd crashed. And he couldn't believe that was an accident.

His vision cleared a little, and he could just barely make out Gracie's face hovering above him. The world around them was dark but some light swathed her face, and he could see every feature.

He had the oddest urge to reach out and touch her face. Touch her hair. Anything to assure himself she was real and here, and that all that worry and fear on her face was for him. *Him.*

I care about you, Will.

Turns out even half-dead after a car accident those words could still haunt and chill him.

"Will, an ambulance is on the way. Don't try

to move. But, can you talk? Say something?" She leaned closer, the wisps of her hair sliding across his cheek, which felt like it had been ripped off.

"Say something to me, please," she whispered, and he thought he saw a few tears slide down her cheeks.

Say something. He had to say something. Make all this stop. She could cry when he was full dead instead of just half.

"Believe me now?" he rasped.

A pained expression crossed her face and she looked up, her face turning into a flashing red light.

"The ambulance is here," she said quietly. "I'm going to go flag them down. Don't—"

But he gripped her arm with the one hand that was functioning and didn't feel like it was being stabbed by a machete. "Don't go." He had the panicked thought that if she left he *would* die, and he found he wasn't quite interested in that prospect.

"I'll get them."

Will didn't know whose voice that was. He only knew it was male and Will didn't particularly care for it. Had she been on a date?

But he didn't have time to dwell on that uncomfortable thought as footsteps and voices surrounded them. Then he was being touched and prodded and moved, and he tried to bite back groans of pain, but he couldn't manage it.

Then he was on a stretcher, being moved and jerked into an ambulance.

"Gracie."

"I'm here," she said, and though he couldn't see her with the paramedics looming over him, a slim, cool hand slid into his.

More voices, more movement, a door slam. And through it all, Gracie's hand held his. Like she'd been doing for the past two years. The only person he'd come to rely on.

"What happened?" she asked gently as a paramedic shined a light into one eye and then the other.

"The brakes and steering went out."

The paramedic worked on him, but Will couldn't seem to force himself to let go of Gracie's hand.

"It wasn't any accident, Gracie. It wasn't."

She didn't say anything to that so he attempted to squeeze her hand, even though it hurt like hell.

"Gracie?"

"Deputy Mosely is looking at your car. There'll be an investigation."

Will snorted, then swallowed down a gasp of pain. "Yeah, I know how those go." He could feel her sigh of a breath against his temple. She moved so he could look at her while the paramedic did something awful to his arm that wasn't holding on to Gracie.

Her big brown eyes were filled with tears and worry, and he wanted to look away from that kind of emotion, but God, it hurt too bad to even close his eyes.

She touched his forehead again, a gentle glide of her fingertips. "Rest. Let's get you better, and then we'll figure out what's going on."

"You don't believe me," he said flatly.

"I don't know what to believe," she returned on a pained whisper.

But it wasn't him. Never him.

Chapter Four

"There's evidence of tampering."

Gracie looked up at Laurel, who stood in the waiting room at the hospital, dressed in her detective khakis and county sheriff's department polo, looking serious and stern.

Believe me now? Will's words kept looping around in her head whether she was dozing or awake while she waited to hear the extent of Will's injuries. Which they wouldn't tell her because she was no one to Will.

"Can you find out how he's doing?"

Laurel smiled thinly. "You know I can't. They're not going to tell you anything, either. Why don't you go home? Get some rest. Come back later."

Gracie shook her head, linking her hands in an effort to keep her composure. If she dug her fingernails into the tops of her hands she could focus on the pinch instead of the guilt swamping her.

She'd been *this* close to deleting his message un-heard, and she just… He would have died. He would have died. He'd be *dead* if she had done that. "What kind of tampering was it?"

"You know I can't tell you that, either." Laurel was firm, but apologetic. If Gracie didn't know Lau-rel as well as she did she might have tried to beg, wheedle or manipulate, but Laurel wouldn't budge. She took her badge more seriously than she took just about everything.

"He's in danger," Gracie said flatly.

"I think that's a safe assumption."

Gracie met Laurel's gaze. "You know what this means."

Laurel sighed. "Not necessarily. If it has some-thing to do with Paula Cooper's crash… It's been years. There was no tampering done to her car back then. There's no evidence this connects at all."

"Yet."

Laurel sighed again and slid into the seat next to Gracie. "I'm going to look into it. If I find a link, I'll investigate it, but you both need to understand this is for the police to figure out."

Gracie knew Laurel was right, but she also knew Will had come to Rightful Claim, told her he'd fig-ured out a pattern and then his car had been tam-pered with. Those couldn't be coincidences.

Laurel would be thorough, Gracie had no doubt.

Even if Laurel wasn't getting married to a Carson, Gracie knew her cousin too well to ever think she'd not follow a lead just because the deceased was a Carson. If there was some connection, Laurel would find it.

Eventually. But Will was in a hospital room with who knew what kind of injuries and Gracie knew she didn't have time for eventually.

"Gracie." Laurel's voice took on a sterner tone. "Promise me you two will let the police handle this."

Gracie didn't want to lie to her cousin, but she also didn't know how she could possibly agree.

"Ms. Delaney?"

Both her and Laurel turned to the nurse, who smiled kindly. Melina knew both of them because their work often brought them to the hospital and since Melina had been Gracie's babysitter once upon a time. "Not you, Deputy. Gracie, Mr. Cooper is able to see visitors now, and he's asked for you, if you'd like to go back."

Gracie hopped to her feet, but so did Laurel.

"I'll need to speak with Mr. Cooper."

Melina nodded. "That'll be fine, but he specifically asked for Gracie. Room 203."

Laurel started striding that way, but Gracie hurried in front of her. "Laurel, listen, I need you to do me a favor."

"I'm here in a professional capacity."

"Please, let me go alone."

"Gracie."

"Please, just… Just give me a few minutes alone. I'm not asking you not to question him, I'm just asking that you let me… Look…" She swallowed at the emotion clogging her throat. "Maybe you don't understand why, but I feel responsible. At least partially. If I'd handled this even remotely differently—"

"You don't know what would have happened."

"Maybe not, but… As my best friend and my cousin and just the best human being I know, please give me five minutes alone with him. Personal minutes."

Laurel sighed heavily. "Five minutes. And I'm right outside the door."

Gracie gave Laurel an impulsive hug. "Thank you." Five minutes wasn't enough really. She'd probably cry when she saw him again. After all, she'd cried in that ambulance. Hopefully Will didn't remember that.

Still, she'd need those few minutes to try to work through all this…stuff. Guilt. Worry. The desperate need to fix what she'd almost irreparably broken.

She and Laurel walked silently to the room number Melina had given them. Laurel gave a little nod and leaned against the wall next to the door. She glanced at her watch meaningfully.

Five minutes. Gracie blew out a breath and knocked on the door before pushing the door open. It was a small room, but the blinds were open to the bright sunshine outside.

Will sat in his bed and slowly turned to look at her as she closed the door behind her. One arm was in a cast, and his face was a maze of bandages. There was a hospital sheet over the bottom half of his body so she couldn't see what kind of damage had been done down there.

He was beat-up and clearly a mess, and still he loomed too large in that bed. Like it didn't matter he'd been pulverized by metal and concrete, he could take it. She almost believed it when he simply sat there and stared at her.

"Hi," she offered from where she stood rooted by the door.

"Hey," he returned, and his voice didn't sound like him at all. She couldn't read his expression, either. Maybe it was just pain.

She walked haltingly to his bedside knowing she had to say whatever it was she was going to say before her five minutes were up and Laurel came in to question him.

He frowned at her as she came to stand beside his bed. "You… You've been here the whole time?"

It was then she realized what he was looking so

quizzically at. The dried blood on her sleeve she'd gotten from touching him out there on that frigid roadside.

When she looked back at his face, he was staring hard at hers.

"You haven't slept," he said, as though that were some great surprise.

"I was waiting to hear... I didn't know how bad off you were. You passed out in the ambulance."

"I don't... I don't remember that. The ambulance."

"What do you remember?"

"Your voice."

Gracie inhaled and then forgot to exhale. It didn't mean anything that she was the thing he remembered. It didn't mean he cared or this mattered, and as guilty as she felt about almost letting him *die*, she couldn't let herself get wrapped up in thinking there was some change here. He was still Will, and she was just...his supplier.

"Gracie." His non-cast arm moved and before she realized what he was doing, he'd taken her hand in his. There was a bandage on top of his hand, and still he gripped her tight. She stared at it.

"Gracie, look at me."

She forced herself to take her gaze off his much bigger, and far more battered, hand squeezing hers.

His blue gaze was earnest and desperate. A look she recognized, and one that made her heart pinch.

Because before last night she would have felt sorry for him, wondered if he needed therapy.

Today, she knew that desperation wasn't out of place, and that maybe, just maybe, Will's obsession with the case wasn't wrong or sad or an attempt not to deal with the complicated feelings about his wife's infidelity or death.

"You have to get me out of here," he said, his gaze never leaving hers. "As soon as possible."

WILL HURT JUST about everywhere and he knew pretty soon a nurse would come in and pump him full of all sorts of crap.

He preferred the pain. The pain kept him centered, and it reminded him of one simple truth.

He'd been right. All along, he'd been right. Whoever Paula had been having an affair with—whether they'd been involved in her death or not—needed to keep it a secret. He didn't know how someone had figured out Will had a clue, but clearly someone had.

Still, Gracie wasn't saying anything. Her hand was limp in his, but she leaned closer. She was a mess. Maybe not physically abused like he currently was, but exhaustion was etched across her sweet face. She had his blood on her shirt and a rip in her jeans. He wondered if it had come from kneeling next to him on the rough asphalt.

He didn't remember much of anything. Not the

crash itself, not the ambulance ride, but he remembered those few seconds of in between where he'd been lying there on fire and freezing at the same time and Gracie suddenly being next to him.

"Will," she whispered. "Laurel is right outside."

He blinked. Then nodded. "We'll discuss it later then."

"There isn't anything to discuss. You have to stay in the hospital till a doctor clears you."

But she still whispered, as if she was afraid her cop cousin was listening. It gave him some hope he could convince her, but it'd have to wait. He was just afraid he didn't have much time.

He *was* hurt, which meant he couldn't fight anyone off. He probably shouldn't drive with his arm in a cast, and hell, he didn't have a car anymore anyway. He'd decided his only chance of survival had been to jump out of the car.

Had he jumped out? He couldn't actually remember it. But they hadn't found him in his car, so he had to have done it.

He lifted his nonbroken arm and pressed fingers to his temple, trying to concentrate on the here and now instead of all the fuzziness around the accident.

Here. Now. He needed help, and Gracie was the only one he could trust. He looked up at her. "You do believe me now, don't you?"

She finally wrapped her fingers around his, just a

slight pressure. "Of course I do. How could I not?" She swallowed, and she lifted her free hand as if to touch him.

He found himself intensely wishing she would, but instead she dropped the hand. "I'm sorry."

"About what?"

"You don't know how close I was to not listening to your message," she said, her voice still a whisper though he didn't think it was about not being heard this time. She looked miserable and devastated. "I was going to delete it. I was cutting you off and it haunts me. If I'd deleted it—"

He hated that look of anguish and guilt on her face. He'd never understood why she'd taken so much of *him* on her shoulders, and he'd never spent much time trying to figure it out. But she'd been helping him for two years, the only actual person who'd stayed a part of his life after Paula's death. She shouldn't feel guilty about anything when she'd been the only one who'd stuck. This girl who had no connection to him prior to telling him his wife had died.

"You would have been right to delete it," Will said firmly. He didn't need her guilt. He needed her help. "I get lost in it all and I don't see beyond it, but you do. You have a life and people who care about you and I know I sound crazy half the time. How could you be as invested in it as me? She wasn't your wife or even anyone you knew."

She studied his face as if she was searching for some particular emotion, but he didn't know what she was looking for, what she wanted. So, he needed to bring the conversation back to where it belonged.

"I need to prove that I'm right. If someone killed her they should pay. There should be some justice."

"You're right. Someone tried to kill *you*. You should have justice, too. And I'm going to help you find it." She held his gaze, bent over him like this, hand still in his. "I promise you, no matter what happens, I'm going to help you find the truth." Her dark eyes blazed with that promise. She had such a certainty about her, such an earnestness. He'd never known anyone quite like her. Dedicated and sweet. She cared about people enough to act on it, enough to help.

He didn't understand her at all, and still she stood over him in this obnoxious hospital bed, her light brown hair glowing near to red in the sunlight streaming through his window. Something fluttered low in his gut, a kind of awareness that prickled over his skin.

He'd noticed before, once or twice, a moment drawn out too long. Noticed the shape of her mouth, or…other parts of her. Exactly like this, a kind of faraway thing that was easy to put out of his mind. They'd always been working on the case. Pictures of Paula's accident or reports about it or... It had always been easy to shift away from that awareness.

Maybe it was the drugs they'd pumped him full of that made it harder to shift now.

But a knock sounded on the door and Gracie all but jumped away from him as if they'd been, well, anything other than just *staring* at each other holding hands.

Laurel Delaney stepped into the room looking very official. Will scowled.

"Mr. Cooper, I need to ask you a few questions."

"About whoever tried to kill me because I got too close to finding the truth?"

He'd give Deputy Delaney credit—she didn't flinch nor did she dig her heels in. She kept that calm, equitable expression on her face and nodded. "There was some evidence of someone tampering with your car. Well, what was left of it."

"Am I supposed to be surprised?"

"Do you have any ideas who might have wanted to cause you harm, Mr. Cooper?"

"Oh, just the man who was having an affair with my wife and probably caused *her* car accident in almost the exact same place."

"Your late wife had no evidence of car tampering. It's also been two years. What would cause someone to come after you now?"

"I found a connection. A clue. It's why I found

Gracie at your party. I told her that I had found something, right there in Rightful Claim. Then we talked
outside. Anyone could have heard me and gotten to
my car."

"So, your theory is we're all living amongst a
killer and have been for two years?"

"Yeah, it is."

Laurel pressed her lips together, clearly irritated
with his steadfast determination. Still, when she
spoke, her voice was even and controlled. "Do you
have any evidence? Anything that might be able to
help us solve this?"

"There was a piece of paper. In my clothes. I'd
written it down." He glanced from Deputy Delaney
to Gracie. "Did they find it?"

The women exchanged a glance and Laurel pulled
a small notebook from her breast pocket. She scrib-
bled a few things on it. "I'm going to see if we can
find a piece of paper. What kind of information does
it have on it?"

"Dates. A few phrases I thought might hint at
where they were meeting. I have the information on
her computer, though." He glanced at Gracie and,
without him even having to ask, she nodded.

"I'll run over and get you some of your things,"
she said.

"You need some sleep," Laurel interrupted.

Gracie opened her mouth, likely to argue, but as

much as Will didn't want to agree with Laurel Delaney, she was right. "You've been here all night. You need to sleep."

"I haven't had parents for twenty years. I know how to take care of myself, thank you very much."

"Gracie—"

She held up her hand at Laurel and Laurel stopped. "Neither of you are in charge of me. Now, I will run over to Will's to grab his computer. Is there anything else you'd like while I'm there?"

Since he'd never once heard Gracie use that firm, don't-you-dare-argue tone, he decided it was best to heed its icy warning. "No, ma'am."

"That's settled then. I'll be back." She turned on a heel and headed for the door, and even though he wanted to say more, he didn't. Because Deputy Delaney was still there, staring at him with that inscrutable cop face.

He knew she didn't believe him. He'd never expected her to, but there being evidence of tampering in his car meant she was going to have to investigate this. She was probably going to get in his way or get him killed in all reality. Because she didn't believe enough of his story to not be a speed bump rather than offer any actual help.

"She has nothing to do with this," Laurel said, nodding to where Gracie had disappeared.

"Excuse me?"

"She has nothing to do with this. If you're in danger, by allowing her to help you, you're putting her in danger. Is that what you want?" He glanced at the door, then back at Laurel.

The thought of Gracie in danger made his stomach turn, because he'd certainly never considered that. But the thought of trying to solve this without her had a flutter of panic settling into his gut. He tried not to let either emotion show on his face. Deputy Delaney didn't need any extra ammunition. "You really think I could stop her?"

Laurel's mouth curved briefly. "You could at least try."

Chapter Five

Gracie drove, white-knuckle against the slick, icy roads, and tried to ignore the way exhaustion was creeping into her. She didn't have time to be hungry, or tired. There was so much to do.

Her mind was so busy going through all the things she needed to accomplish—first and foremost convincing Will he needed to stay put in the hospital until his doctors cleared him—she didn't notice tire tracks in the snowy road until she was almost halfway up the mountain to Will's cabin.

It had snowed last night. There shouldn't be any tracks leading up here because any tracks Will had made coming down last night would have been mostly filled—not deep and fresh.

Someone had tampered with Will's car, enough so he'd had to jump out of the vehicle to save himself. It could only be a very bad sign that there were tracks leading up to his cabin now so soon after.

The problem was there wasn't really anywhere to stop or turn around, not with how icy and narrow the winding mountain road was. But if someone was up there, someone who'd purposefully hurt Will, Gracie didn't think it would be best for her to head up there, either.

She studied the road, the snow, the way her truck was beginning to lose traction as she eased off the accelerator. She needed to find a place to stop, to gather her thoughts.

There was a slight flat spot on the curve, though it would mean parking perilously close to a very steep drop off, and she wasn't 100 percent sure her truck would fit the small space. But it was the only choice. *The only choice.*

She repeated those three words to herself as she navigated her truck toward the flat patch. She had to fight the urge to squeeze her eyes shut when the tires skidded on the ice. She gripped the steering wheel harder no matter how badly her hands were beginning to ache, and she carefully tapped the brake as she moved closer and closer to that awful edge.

It took a full minute to realize the truck had stopped and she was no longer moving forward or sideways. She was safe and still, right on the edge of the road.

She swallowed, breathed and then slowly peeled

her hands off the steering wheel, wincing at the pain in her joints. But she was okay. Parked and okay.

She turned off the engine, studying the tire tracks that led up and around the last curve before Will's cabin came into view. She kept her gaze on the curve as she reached over and blindly pawed through her purse for her phone.

She pulled up Laurel's entry and hit Call and only when Laurel answered did Gracie remember to breathe.

But at the same time Laurel spoke her greeting, the front of a car appeared on that curve, coming down. Gracie dove across the seats, losing her phone in the process. She lay there hoping they'd mistake her truck as abandoned. There was no way they'd miss it parked here, but they'd have a hard time stopping their own car, especially going *down* the slick road. Of course, they'd gone up it at some point and—

A loud bang almost simultaneous with the sound of breaking glass had Gracie shrieking as shards of driver's-side window shattered over her. She wanted to scream again, but she had enough presence of mind to know she had to be quiet. She had to focus.

The car hadn't moved, so she could only assume the bang and breaking of glass hadn't been them crashing into her, but them shooting at her.

The motor of the other car was still running and

Gracie tried to focus on that. She didn't know how many people there were in the vehicle, but surely they'd have to stop for any of them to get out. Were they stopped?

But she listened, eyes squeezed shut, body frozen in its prone position across the front seats. The engine got quieter and quieter until she could barely hear it at all.

Oh God, had they left? Just shot and left?

Please God.

She decided it was safe to move, though she didn't get out of the truck yet. They could have left men behind. That could have been a warning and they were going to turn around at the bottom and come back up. She had no idea who it was or what they were after, so she could only try to protect herself as best she could.

Find her phone, then try to get to Will's cabin. Maybe on foot. She wasn't too far away and she could get into Will's place and find his rifle. It wasn't foolproof, but it was the best she could do.

She peered down at the floor of the truck and grabbed her phone. The previous call had ended, but Gracie redialed Laurel's number as she carefully maneuvered back into a sitting position. She glanced at where the car had to have gone, and didn't see or hear anyone returning, so she pushed out of her truck and onto the snowy road.

"I have two county deputies headed toward Will's cabin," Laurel said by way of greeting. "What the hell is going on? Did you crash, too?"

"No. I... Someone drove down from Will's cabin and shot my car."

"Shot? Jesus, Gracie, did you call 911?"

"No, it just broke my window. I'm fine." She stumbled a little bit in a drift of snow as she tried to jog the distance to Will's cabin.

"Someone is shooting at you. You're not fine. This is not fine."

"I parked on the road and I'm walking up to the cabin. Hang up with me and tell your deputies to stop anyone going down this road. I'm going to hole up in Will's cabin, with his rifle, and wait for someone to give me a ride home. I'll deal with my broken window later." But Laurel wasn't listening. Gracie could hear her talking to someone else.

"I've radioed them to stop anyone coming down from that road, but did you get a look at the car? Color? Make? Anything?"

Gracie tried to think back to the brief glimpse of car she'd seen before she'd dived across the seats. "I can't... I don't know. I didn't get a good look. I tried to hide."

"That's fine. That road shouldn't have any traffic on it, and as long as we're not too late someone will stop him. Now, you—"

Gracie smelled the smoke before she saw it. At first she didn't think much of it. It was winter. Fireplaces or bonfires or— But then she saw the smoke and broke out into a dead run, ignoring Laurel's words in her ears.

The cabin came into view and Gracie gasped. "Call the fire department."

"Gracie, what—"

"I have to see what I can save."

"Gracie!"

But she couldn't listen to Laurel tell her it was dangerous. She clicked the phone off and stared at Will's pretty little cabin up in flames. Whatever evidence he'd collected over the years likely going up with it.

She couldn't let that happen.

WILL KNEW HE was being an ass to the nurses. He felt a modicum of guilt, but no one would let him out of here and he didn't think that was legal. The only thing keeping him in this obnoxious bed was the fact he wasn't quite desperate enough to rip the IV out of his arm.

He eyed the needle attached to his broken arm. Surely it couldn't be that difficult to take it off. He peeled one side of the tape off, but before he could start experimenting with medical equipment removal, his door flew open.

Not gently or with a knock like the nurses did either, and visiting hours were over. Gracie had never returned with his computer, but he figured she'd taken a much-needed nap and he'd get his hands on it tomorrow.

Instead, Gracie stumbled into his room as if she'd been pushed, and he frowned because there were black smudges over the same clothes she'd been wearing this morning. It looked like she'd had the same black on her face and tried to wash it off but instead left a streaky kind of gray complexion.

Laurel was behind her looking furious.

"What's going on?" he demanded.

Laurel jerked her chin at him. "Tell him," she ordered.

Gracie heaved a sigh, looking at her feet, then the window, anywhere but at him or Laurel.

"There was a bit of an incident," Gracie said cryptically.

"What the hell does that mean?"

"Well, when I got to your cabin…" She cleared her throat. "It was on fire."

He struggled to sit up straighter. "Fire. What? I don't…"

"She's leaving out quite a few pieces of the story," Laurel said, anger and frustration written on every line of her face. Which was weird, because mostly he'd only ever seen Laurel cool and calm and detached. Cop-like. This was not any of those things.

"I drove up to your cabin, and when I got there—"

"Before she got there a strange vehicle came down the mountain from your cabin, shot at *her*—"

"At my car. I don't think they saw me."

Laurel flung her arms up in the air, as agitated as he'd ever seen the woman. "I can't believe you're being so ridiculous. You are too smart for this, Gracie Delaney."

"You are overreacting, *Laurel Delaney*. My God, I am a grown woman and—"

"Someone needs to tell me what the hell is going on," Will demanded.

"—you can't boss me around anymore. I'm not your ward and I never was."

"I am not trying to boss you around. I'm your cousin. I love you. You—"

"Ladies," he said fiercely.

"—were reckless and foolish and you need some damn sleep."

"I will—"

Finally he used his fingers to whistle as long and as loud as he could. Both women glared at him, but at least they'd stopped yelling over each other.

"I want an explanation and I want it now since apparently my house was *on fire* and Gracie is covered in…" His brain clicked to the most horrible thought possible. "You weren't in the cabin, were you?"

"Well, not…not exactly."

"Stop talking in riddles," he said between clenched teeth, grasping the IV tower to fight the impulse to cross the room and give her a little shake.

"When I saw the cabin was on fire, I… Well, I carefully poked around to see if I could get to your comp—"

"You did what?" Will demanded, jumping out of bed.

"Sit down," Gracie and Laurel ordered in unison.

He didn't sit down, but he didn't move toward them since he was in a ridiculous hospital gown. He stood next to his bed, furious, and holding on to the damn IV tower with everything he had.

"What possessed you to risk your life for *anything* in that place?" he said, doing his best to speak normally instead of a growl. It didn't go so well.

Gracie turned to Laurel. "Would you give us a few minutes alone?" When Laurel only scowled, Gracie reached out and squeezed her cousin's arm. "Please."

Laurel huffed out a breath. "Fine. But I'm right outside, and in ten minutes you are done here. Ten minutes and we are getting you some dinner and a bed to sleep in."

Gracie nodded, then just stood there as Laurel marched out of the hospital room. Finally she turned to face him, a paltry smile curving her lips. "So, how are you?"

She was standing there covered in black soot. She'd been... He could picture it all too well and it made him sick to his stomach. "What were you thinking?"

"It was your evidence. Two years of your life. I was careful. I'm not stupid. But I had to try."

"This isn't your fight. You shouldn't have... You shouldn't have done that, Gracie. It was just things. You could've..." So many could'ves and they all horrified him down to his soul.

"What does it matter?" she asked, and it finally clicked why her voice sounded all wrong. She'd inhaled smoke.

What did it matter? She'd risked herself and... "It matters. Of course it matters."

"Why? You don't care about me."

She could've shot him for the force of that blow. "Gracie," he exhaled.

"I'm not saying you actively wish me harm, but I'm kind of nothing to you. A means to an end. So I was being your means, and in the end I didn't do anything. I couldn't get to the computer." She shrugged, and he couldn't read her at all. "So, I don't know why you're scolding me or why it matters."

He could only stand there and stare at her. She wasn't making any sense, and he just wanted...

He just… There was something all twisted up in his chest or his gut and he couldn't unwind it. He couldn't make sense of how much he didn't like her saying *you don't care about me.*

"I did what I had to do," she continued in that same maddeningly even voice, like this wasn't messed up. "I was careful. I don't need scolding or disapproval. I'm a grown woman. You should be more concerned about the fact someone burned your cabin down."

"I'm more concerned about the fact someone shot at you and then you decided to run into a burning building."

She folded her arms across her chest, her nose going up in the air. "Those are gross exaggerations."

Screw the hospital gown. He crossed the room because maybe erasing the space between them would help him make sense of her.

But she was standing there, soot covered and exhaustedly pale. "You will not risk your safety for this. Do you understand me?"

"What I understand is you're not the boss of me, Will. You're not the anything of me."

That horrible knot in his chest only tied tighter and sharper. It didn't make sense. *She* didn't make sense. His hand itched to…do something, touch her or…something. Which also didn't make sense and so he just stood there frozen and confused. Something like anger starting to work through him.

"You know what? I don't care. I don't care if I'm not your boss or in charge of you or what, you won't dare risk your life for this again. Period. This is my thing and whoever this person is, he's after *me*. You won't be hurt in this. I won't allow it. Go home. Get some sleep and… You'll stay away from me until this is solved."

"Like hell."

Something inside of him snapped, that tight knot maybe. Because he stepped closer. So close their noses were almost touching and he could see the darker flecks of brown in her eyes. "Get it through your head that I cannot bear the thought of you being hurt by this."

She stared up at him, though something in her posture softened. Then she reached out. If he wasn't so churned up or whatever he might have sidestepped her cool, small hand pressing against his cheek.

It was nearly impossible to breathe through that. All those tight knots inside him loosened, but the spaces filled with something else. Something familiar and dangerous and he shoved it all away and used his good hand to pull hers off his face.

But he didn't let her hand go. It seemed odd her hands were so small when she was such a force. So strong and determined, but her hand in his felt fragile somehow. So he met her gaze, and that didn't help him understand anything that was happening, but at least it gave him her to focus on.

"Go home. Get some sleep. Be safe, my God. But you need rest. You know you do."

She swallowed. "Okay, on one condition. You promise you'll stay put. Do what the doctors say. Don't try to get out of here. Not without me. Please."

He glanced at the IV stand, then her hand in his again. He had to get out of here. He knew he did, but… "Okay." He squeezed her hand. As much as he needed to get out of here, he needed her, too. "I promise."

Chapter Six

Gracie would admit to precisely no one she felt like she was going to pass out and throw up at the same time.

She stepped out of Will's hospital room, and maybe she could blame the dazed double vision on the fact Will had voluntarily touched her. He'd taken her hand and squeezed it and made a promise to her and...

She was probably hallucinating, really.

"I don't want you going back to your house," Laurel said, popping up out of seemingly nowhere. "It's not safe."

"They or he or whoever it was didn't see me."

"They saw your truck. Which Vanessa has taken care of by the way."

"A Carson is taking care of my truck? Vanessa Carson at that?"

Laurel wrinkled her nose. "I know, but she promised to be on her best behavior. I would have had Cam do it, but I gave him a different job."

"Laurel, please tell me you didn't."

But Laurel didn't tell her anything. She led her to the entrance of the hospital and there was Cam, Laurel's brother, freshly home from a stint as a marine.

"I don't need a bodyguard. Cousin or otherwise," Gracie grumbled.

"And here I was hoping to get some practice in," Cam replied. For as military as he appeared on the outside, Gracie had grown up with him. Cam was strong and somewhat detached, but he was kind. All the Delaney cousins had made her feel welcome and part of the family even when their parents hadn't.

"Cam's going to start a security business now that he's home for good."

"That's great," Gracie replied, trying not to seem ungrateful. She smiled at Cam. "I don't need security."

"The shot-out window on your vehicle says otherwise," Cam replied gently. "It isn't safe for you to be alone until Laurel determines what's going on. I'm going to take you to your place to gather your things, then we'll head to the Delaney Ranch."

"If I'm not safe, why would you bring me home? I'm not sure your father would care for that."

"Dad can deal," Laurel said firmly. "I've already

told him as such. I've also told Cam to bar the door to your bedroom until you've slept eight hours."

"I don't like this," Gracie said firmly. But exhaustion had stolen her will to fight or do much of anything.

"Feed her before she sleeps," Laurel instructed Cam.

Gracie figured she must be really be exhausted because she couldn't even work up a comment about how she didn't need someone forcing her to eat. She could only follow Cam out to his truck.

Cam said something, but Gracie yawned and couldn't make it out. The next thing she knew, she startled awake in a dark room. The bed was comfortable and something about it all was familiar.

But she didn't remember getting here. She didn't remember anything from the hospital parking lot on.

Her phone chimed and she realized that's what had woken her up. She glanced at the time on her phone screen. Five in the morning. Which meant she'd actually slept something like twelve hours if not more. The light of the phone also gave her a clue as to where she was.

The Delaney Ranch. When her parents had died, she'd bounced around from family member to family member until fifth grade. Then she'd landed at the Delaney Ranch with her four cousins and had stayed through high school.

Though her cousins had been great, Gracie'd had no illusions Uncle Geoff considered her one of his own. Even if she was his late brother's only child.

Gracie scrubbed her hands over her face and tried to focus her brain on the present. Text message. Someone had texted her. At five in the morning?

She opened the message. From Will.

Meet me at my cabin.

She frowned at her phone. Will had promised to stay put. He had promised. Why would he be at the cabin before the sun even rose and when it had been on fire not all that long ago? Besides, he didn't have a car. His had been totaled. How would he have gotten there?

Something didn't add up and she needed to figure it out.

Coffee. Good lord, she needed coffee. And food. She got out of bed and stumbled to the door. It was weird, as many years as she'd spent living at the Delaney Ranch, it had never felt like home. She'd been a permanent guest at best.

On a sigh, she headed for the kitchen. The smell of food and coffee about made her whimper.

When Gracie stepped into the kitchen, her cousin Jen was standing in front of the big stove, humming all too happily for 5:00 a.m. She turned and smiled at Gracie. "I'd hoped you'd sleep longer."

Gracie only grunted. Jen moved to the coffee maker and poured a generous mug before sliding it in front of Gracie. "You just let me know when you're functioning. Cam's doing some kind of recon nonsense. Dylan and Dad are doing the ranch chores." She frowned. "Dad's been acting so weird this week," she muttered.

"He doesn't want me here."

Jen waved it away. A few minutes later she put a plate full of eggs, bacon and toast slathered in butter in front of Gracie.

"Have I ever told you I love you with all my heart?"

Jen grinned. "Not since you lived here and I made you breakfast back then."

Gracie dove into the breakfast and coffee and felt almost human once she was finished. But feeling human meant figuring out what was going on with that cryptic text message.

"Do you know where Laurel is?"

"Sleeping, hopefully. But she has to be back at it tonight, and she did say you could wake her up if it's important."

"No. That's fine. I don't suppose you have a car I could borrow?"

"Sorry. I've got to be at the store at seven, but I

can drop you off somewhere. Cam could probably pick you up whenever you need another ride."

"Cam and Laurel didn't insist you keep me here till I have some kind of shadow?"

Jen laughed. "Of course they did. I'm just not listening."

Gracie chuckled, but it died as she stared at the text message on her phone again.

Surely Will wasn't up at that burned-down cabin freezing his butt off waiting for her. He wouldn't have broken his promise to her. She really hoped.

"Can you drop me off at the hospital?"

"Sure, but they're not going to let you in to see Will at this hour."

"I know, but I'd rather wait there than here. I don't want to run into your dad. Sorry."

"*I'm* sorry," Jen replied.

"Don't be. You're perfect and my favorite person right about now."

"How about some more food?"

Gracie frowned at her phone. Something wasn't right. But if Will had broken his promise… "Sure, I'll take a little more."

WILL STARED AT the needle in his arm. He'd promised Gracie he'd stay put, but it was almost seven in the morning and how long could he be expected to reasonably keep a promise?

Someone had tried to kill him. Someone had burned down his cabin, and all the evidence he'd compiled over two years trying to figure out who his wife had been sleeping with was certainly gone.

Which meant he *had* to be so close. Or at least they thought he was. But what had he done differently in the days leading up to his car being tampered with that might lead someone to think he knew?

The only thing he could think of was going into Rightful Claim. Had someone in that bar heard him talk to Gracie and assumed he'd come up with the killer's identity? Panicked and messed with his car? What exactly had he said that night? All he remembered was telling her he had new information.

And her telling him she cared about him.

But that wasn't important right now. What was important was someone must have overheard that conversation and thought he had more information than he did.

No matter how often he tried to tell himself to be methodical and rational when working this all out, the only reason to tamper with his car, burn his cabin, shoot at Gracie—*Christ*—was they had killed Paula in the first place. An affair wasn't a big enough thing to cover up with murder, but murder certainly was.

Which meant he couldn't be stuck here. Both a sitting duck and ineffective when someone was out there trying to get rid of him and all his stuff. When someone had shot at Gracie, who had nothing to do with this. Not really.

Keeping his promise to her was only putting her in more danger. Yeah. Exactly. He ignored the pit of guilt and began to pick the edge of the tape on his arm.

Again, just as he was getting somewhere, the door opened.

Gracie stepped in, but stopped short at the sight of him. "You're here," she said, frowning.

"Of course I'm here. Where else would I be?" He surreptitiously smoothed the tape back into place.

She looked down at the phone she was holding in one hand. "Did you text me a few hours ago?"

"Text you? What? I don't even have my phone. Laurel said they didn't uncover any of my belongings from the accident. Burned or lost in the snow."

Gracie's eyes widened and she let out a whoosh of breath.

"What's going on?" he demanded.

She took a few careful steps toward his bed. "Or maybe your stuff was taken," she said gravely. "Someone texted me from your number at five this morning asking me to meet them at the cabin." She held out the screen to him and he squinted at the text.

Meet me at my cabin.

"Someone has my phone and is trying to lure you to them." He flung the blankets off his body. Luckily they'd let him change into regular clothes last night so he didn't feel completely ridiculous, even if they were too-big sweats someone had left him at Gracie's behest. Because his clothes were burned up. "We have to get out of here."

"You haven't been cleared."

"They said they might release me today. We're just speeding it up a bit. Gracie, someone is after me. Actually, no, worse. Someone is after *you*."

"I think I've survived a little better than you have," she said, gesturing at his cast and IV and probably him in general.

"I won't give them a chance to do to you what they've done to me."

Dark brown eyes studied him with a kind of emotion he could only guess at. Something like hope, a warmth he hadn't seen from anyone else in years. For *years*, Gracie had been his only source of good.

If she'd felt pity for him, she'd hidden it well. Or maybe her pity didn't suffocate like the town's pity had when he'd still lived down there.

"Laurel has my cousin basically bodyguarding me. Sort of. I may have slipped away this morning."

"Don't slip away again," he said firmly. "Let someone watch out for you." He pointed to the phone still in her hand. "Someone is trying to lure you to an isolated spot, and using me to do it. You need to be protected." He didn't like the idea of this random cousin protecting her, but she was a Delaney. She had a million people on her side, and he had to trust that.

Her eyebrows drew together. "Who will protect you?"

Protect him? He'd never had anyone protecting him. Not really. He'd never known his dad, and for as long as he could remember his mom had been the one in need of protection from a string of men who'd always taken advantage of her. Then she'd married Phil and basically washed her hands of her useless son. He'd had Paula by then, and even though he couldn't believe his wife had *never* loved him, it hadn't lasted. Not the way it was supposed to.

"Will."

He shook his head. This was all ancient history. He needed to focus on a little more current history. Who was after him? What kind of man had been sleeping with his wife? "It doesn't matter. I don't need protecting," he muttered, trying to turn away.

But Gracie grabbed his good arm. "It matters to me. We're in this together, Will. You're in danger." She frowned down at her phone before shoving it into her coat pocket. "And I guess it's possible I'm in danger, too." She let her hand drop from his arm.

"Which is why—"

"We protect each other." She stood there, fierce

warrior that she always was. It amazed him, the weight this tiny woman carried on her shoulders, how that sweet, soft demeanor could fool a person into thinking there was no steel underneath.

But he remembered, quite clearly, the day she'd come to his door to tell him Paula was dead. A quiet determination. A sense of purpose. A strength he'd envied when it felt like his world had been pulled out from under him.

"Then you have to get me out of here. I can't sit here and wait around. I have to get out there and figure out what's going on. I don't care if the police *are* looking into it this time. I'm the one who's been looking into it for two years. Paula's lover might have destroyed my evidence, but he can't destroy the things I know. I just have to work out the puzzle."

"*We*, Will," she said resolutely. "*We*."

"So, you'll get me out?"

"First, you have to understand and accept you can't shut me out of this. If I help you get out of here, then you are stuck with me until this is over. Cam and Laurel won't be happy with me, but they can't… Laurel can't bend the rules and Cam won't."

"But you will?"

"If you promise me we're in this together? Yes. I know Laurel did everything she could with Paula's case, but sometimes even our best isn't enough. You're right. You have the most evidence, the most stake. They're bound by rules. I don't have to be. But that doesn't mean we should work against them. I'm going to text Laurel about your number texting me. We want them investigating, too. We're just going to investigate…our way. Together."

He didn't want to risk her, but he couldn't do this alone, either. Not with a broken arm. She was the only one he trusted. She was the only one he had, and that wasn't just because of the circumstances he'd been living in the past year. It was her. Her strength and steadfastness and support.

He'd just have to be strong enough and smart enough to protect her, for as long as he needed her. He held out his arm with the IV needle in it. "All right. We're in this together."

She smiled and nodded, pulling her phone out. She typed in a text to Laurel about the phantom text message, then shoved the phone back in her pocket. "Okay, so how do we get out of here?"

"First, you're going to have to pull this out of me," he instructed.

She looked at the needle grimly, but she nodded. "Don't look."

Chapter Seven

"Crap," Gracie muttered.

"What?" Will demanded. His eyes were still squeezed shut even though she'd removed the IV needle a full minute ago. She'd even bandaged it up with a Band-Aid she'd found in one of the cabinets.

"I don't have a car." She released his hand reluctantly. "The IV is out. You can open your eyes."

He opened his eyes and looked down at where the IV had once been attached to his arm. "Not bad, coroner."

She smiled a little at that. "I may be used to working on dead bodies, but I do know something about basic bandaging. My car is at Carson Auto. I can't get it without Laurel or Cam finding me. It might not even be fixed yet."

"We have to try."

Gracie glanced at her watch. Surely Cam had found out Jen had given her a ride over to the hospital by now. He'd be mad and he'd be here any second. But Will was right: they had to try.

Gracie believed in doing things the right way, but she'd been willing to make exceptions for Will. Laurel would never approve of this. She'd want them to sit tight and wait and let the police do their jobs.

But sometimes the right way didn't get the truth. Clearly, since Paula's death had been ruled an accident. Gracie would have to leave Laurel and Cam and their rules behind if she wanted to help Will right now.

"We won't go out the front exit." She frowned at him. "You need a jacket."

"I'll live."

"It's December. You're injured. You need a jacket."

"Where are you going to find me one?"

That was a good question. There weren't any places in town that sold winter coats. Fairmont would be the closest place they could go for one. She could go prowling the hospital for unattended coats, but they didn't have time and she didn't want to draw attention to herself.

Her phone buzzed and she glanced at it, bracing for another text from Will's number. But this number was worse.

Cam.

If you're not in my truck, which is parked outside the main entrance, in three minutes, you will be sorry.

She had no doubt. But Cam waiting for her outside did give her an idea.

"We're going to have to be sneaky. And I'm going to feel super guilty about it, but it's the only way."

"Fine with me. Just save the guilt for once it's done."

Gracie nodded, but she couldn't help wincing as she typed up the lie.

Can you come up to Will's room instead? With an extra coat if you've got one. He lost his in the fire and they're going to let him out this afternoon.

Will read over her shoulder with a frown. "He's not going to help us. I can guarantee you that."

"No, but he might bring you a coat. I'm going to meet him in the lobby and ask him for the keys. I'm going to tell him to bring you the coat. While he does that, I'm going to move his truck to the back entrance, and you meet me there as soon as he leaves."

"Wow, that *is* sneaky. I'm impressed."

"What can I say? I'm an evil genius. Now it's your turn. We have to figure out where the heck we're going to go."

Will swore under his breath.

"Precisely. Get to thinking. I bet you have less than ten minutes all told." She shoved her phone into her pocket then forced herself to smile at Will. "Let's just hope this works."

He rubbed his good hand over his chin as he studied her, and something about the study was…different. Not his usual baffled *what is with you* or his calculating attempts to try to get her to do something. This was almost like he wanted to understand some piece of her.

She was clearly hallucinating.

"Good luck," he muttered.

Gracie nodded and headed for the door. "Back exit. Soon as he leaves. Or we're toast."

"Aye aye, Captain."

She didn't look back. Couldn't allow herself the precious seconds. She had to be in the lobby before Cam got to Will's room. She jogged down the hallway, then paused to make herself look calm and ambling before she pushed out the doors into the lobby.

Cam was already halfway across the room. He looked furious, but he had an old work coat swung over his arm.

"You're lucky I'm more pissed at Jen than I am at you."

"I only came to the hospital. I don't see what the big deal is."

"Do you recall someone shooting at you yesterday?"

"Not *at* me, per se."

His scowl deepened and Gracie hadn't thought that possible. "How can you be this resolutely obtuse?"

"Years of practice," she muttered. "Anyway, why don't you take the coat up to Will, huh?"

Cam's scowl morphed into something softer. "Why can't you take it up to him?"

Gracie tried to hide her wide-eyed surprise at his very reasonable question. "I can't… I can't…" Cam's eyes narrowed suspiciously, but Gracie knew at least one of Cam's weaknesses. Distressed female emotion.

She sniffled and looked away, working up looking emotional and hurt. If she pretended that she was upset over Will she had no doubt Cam would rush to do what she asked without demanding answers about what was going on. "Trust me, you don't want to know," she said in a wavering voice.

Cam grimaced. "Do I need to break his other arm?"

"No. Just…" She took a deep shaky breath, hoping she wasn't overselling it. "Give him his coat and let's go, please. I'd like to wait in your truck, though. They might let him out and I just… I can't…" She made a little noise, hoping it sounded like a sob.

"All right." He handed over the keys, looking supremely uncomfortable. "At least pay attention to your surroundings. Someone could be out there, Gracie. Someone *is* after you."

Gracie nodded, keeping her gaze averted in the hopes he thought she was crying.

He muttered something but he headed for the hallway to Will's room. She tried to walk at a normal pace toward the front entrance, but once she got out the doors she broke into a dead run toward Cam's truck parked in the very front.

She wasn't totally foolish. She looked around to make sure no one was following her. But she didn't think whoever had tried to kill Will knew much about *her.* Especially if she wasn't in her shot-out car.

Adjusting the seat so she could reach the pedals, she started the ignition at the same time. She peeled out of the parking spot and drove as quickly and safely as she could to the back of the hospital.

For every second that ticked by, she worried about what could happen. Cam could stop Will. A doctor could stop Will. Whoever was after him could intercept him in the hospital and really, truly harm him.

When the panic breathing came, she started counting through it. She would have made a terrible cop on a stakeout because she was ready to run screaming into the hospital, and when she glanced at the time on her phone she realized she'd been sitting here for no more than two minutes.

But those minutes crept by until her nerves were strung so tight she was one second away from turning off the truck and marching inside.

But that was when Will appeared out the back exit. Well, a lump in a coat that looked like the one Cam had been holding stepped out the door, but he walked right to Cam's truck and opened the passenger-side door.

He struggled a little bit while getting in, his injuries clearly hampering his mobility. Gracie tried not to let that worry her even more than she was already.

"So, where are we going?" she asked once he was seated and was struggling to fasten his seat belt.

"Let's head toward Fairmont for now," he said through gritted teeth, clearly in pain. So much so he was pale with it.

But she couldn't be distracted by pain or worry. Couldn't be distracted by the fact Cam would be furious, and might even stop her if she didn't get out of here now.

"Hold on to your hat," she offered before gunning the accelerator.

WILL TRIED TO think through the throbbing pain in every part of his body as Gracie drove far too fast down the highway to Fairmont. Past the scene of his accident, and then Paula's. It was strange to watch those places fly by knowing nothing was left of either wreck.

"Your cousin is going to come looking for his truck." Will felt the need to point it out.

"I know."

"Laurel probably already has county on our tails."

"She's not on duty until tonight," Gracie replied in that breezy way she had when she was lying about something.

"Okay, so say we make it to Fairmont undetected. Then what?" He winced as a bump had him hitting his elbow against the car door and jarring his broken arm.

"Then we… Well, I don't know. I got us out of the hospital. You come up with the rest." She heaved out a breath. "I'm having second thoughts, Will. What are we going to solve by running away?"

"We're not running away," he said firmly. "I mean *I* am running away from being stuck in that hospital, but we're not running away from the problem. We need somewhere to hunker down and think and…"

There were almost no businesses along the highway from Bent to Fairmont. Not even a gas station. But they'd just passed a sign for a motel two miles off the highway.

"Turn around."

"What?" Gracie demanded.

"Turn around and turn left at that sign."

"Why?" But she was slowing down. She reached a center divider and got onto the opposite side of the highway.

"There's a motel there. Off the highway. It might buy us some time since Cam and Laurel probably assume we've either gone to your place or Fairmont. They won't guess a motel." He had to hope.

"But why a motel?"

"I want to see if Paula ever stopped here."

Gracie was quiet after that, following the signs for the motel. The road toward it was windy and hidden, and there was a good chance no one would find them back here. It would buy them some time.

"I'm going to park the truck in this back lot just in case," Gracie said, pulling onto a patch of gravel behind the motel that was probably there for employees.

It was a squat sprawling building. Ramshackle at best. It may have been white once, but now it was just grayish brown—a mix of peeling paint and snow and mud. A few windows that had apparently been broken had been repaired with duct tape.

Will couldn't imagine his put-together late wife ever coming to a place like this. She would have run screaming in the opposite direction before ever parking. At least, that's what he'd thought, but he'd never imagined her an adulterer. But the mysterious "night" meetings, the coming home smelling like someone else, the giggling text messages she refused to show him.

He'd let a lot of it continue without confrontation for too long because he hadn't wanted to believe it. Not just the affair, but that everything he'd thought was true about her was a lie.

Gracie turned off the ignition and turned to face him. He couldn't exactly read her thoughts, but clearly she thought he was crazy. What else was new?

"What are we going to accomplish here?" she asked gently. The kind of gentle he didn't like from anyone, let alone her.

"I don't know who's after us or why, but I'm sure it has to do with the affair. If we can piece together the affair, then we can piece together what happened that night she died. And there's no way everything that happened in the past two days doesn't connect to that."

"I don't think you're wrong exactly, but… We're in danger. You especially. The further we dig into this, the more in danger we are."

"I know. And I hate that you're in danger because of me, but we can't go back now. We're already here in danger. Now, the only choice we have is to figure it out before they hurt you."

"Us. Hurt *us*."

"Look, Gracie…" He didn't know how to articulate

what he wanted to say. "You shouldn't worry about me. Keeping you safe is our number one priority."

"Why would you be less of a priority than me?"

"We don't have time to argue," he muttered, moving to push open the car door.

"Then don't argue. Our safety is the number one priority. And for what it's worth, I can't find an argument for the theory it connects to the cheating, but I also know it isn't easy to… Well, you didn't want to know who the guy was."

"No, I didn't." Sometimes Will forgot Gracie had been there in those first dark days. So much so he wasn't even sure of all the things he might have laid at a stranger's feet when he'd been so blasted off his feet by her unexpected death.

He'd built himself up to a confrontation. To demand to know why she'd betrayed him. Instead, he'd gotten Gracie on his doorstep informing him Paula was dead.

He didn't have time to go back there. He had to move forward. "I didn't want to know much of anything about what an idiot I was when I was still in the midst of it, but I do want to know who killed her. I want there to be some justice for that. There's no reason to take these drastic measures against us if someone didn't kill her."

"Yeah, I think you're right, but…" Gracie looked

at the building in front of them. "What are we looking for here?"

"We'll go in and ask if anyone knew Paula or remembers anything about her." Something he'd avoided for too long. He'd spent two years poring over records and emails and *things*. He'd never wanted to deal with people who might question why he needed answers for the death of a woman who'd been cheating on him.

There was no answer with that question, or, if there was, he didn't want to find it. He'd never wanted to find it.

But he couldn't hide anymore. He couldn't keep shying away from hard questions people might ask when Gracie's life was in danger.

"I'm sorry this is happening to you, Will. It isn't fair," she offered, apparently mistaking his hesitation for trepidation over the unfairness of it all. When in fact he was afraid he'd forgotten how to be a person who dealt with other people.

"Life isn't fair," he returned resolutely. Because it was true. Life had never been fair, so whether he knew how to be with people or not anymore, he had to do it. He reached for the door handle, wincing as he remembered that he wasn't sturdy or healthy. He had a broken arm and a million bruises.

"Let me open the door for you," Gracie said, already hopping out of the truck.

"No. You're not going to treat me like an invalid, broken arm or not." He got the door open himself before Gracie could hurry over and do it for him. He got out of the truck, trying to hide the shudder of pain that went through him when his boots landed on gravel.

He stood there in the parking lot for a second just breathing in the frigid Wyoming air. Everything hurt, body and soul, but he wasn't dead, even though someone had tried to kill him. And more important, Gracie was here, and he had to do everything in his power to protect her.

"I could do the asking. I can handle this and you can stay here," Gracie offered hopefully.

"You're the one who told me we were in this together, Gracie. That means no one stays behind. Besides, maybe she never stayed here. It's not her kind of place, that's for sure. And if she did, it'll be good for me to know. It's been a long time."

"Why is it good for you to know how awful she was? She's dead and it shouldn't matter. You're alive and good, and everything she did to you was wrong."

"But not wrong enough to die over."

"No, I know, but—"

"Paula might be dead, and drudging up the affair stuff might suck, but as much as I need to find out who killed her, I need to learn from my mistakes. You asked me what I thought would happen after I found out the truth, what would be next, and to be honest I don't have a clue. But something will have to change." He strode toward the motel, the strangest sense of purpose washing over him. Not that obsessive, driving need to find out what was right, as if answers would magically fix the broken things inside him.

An end. So he could have a new beginning.

Gracie fell into step next to him. "Her cheating on you wasn't your fault, so I don't think you need to learn anything."

Will smiled ruefully. "Maybe it wasn't my fault per se, but I wasn't a very good husband."

"How could anyone be a good husband to someone who could do what she did?"

Even though Gracie looked fairly young, he didn't often think of her that way. She had such a confidence and strength about her that often had him thinking she was older than she was. But the truth was that as much death as Gracie had seen in her job, she was still quite a few years younger than him and clearly had lived the kind of life that led you to believe in the goodness of other people.

All he had in him anymore was distrust. And something like, well, he didn't like the word *fear* because it seemed cowardly, but there was a certain amount of discomfort at the thought of letting anyone into his life. Clearly he didn't have the right instinct when it came to people.

He looked at the woman pulling the front door open. Maybe Gracie was the one exception to that. He might always be wrong about people, he might be a distant, warped human being these days, but he couldn't deny Gracie's goodness. Who could?

That was not why he was here though. He was here to solve a problem. Keep Gracie safe and figure out who'd killed Paula.

The order in which he thought of those two things was weird, but he didn't have time to consider it. He stepped inside. It smelled like cigarette smoke and maybe mildew or mold. Gracie wrinkled her nose and again Will was struck by how wrong this all was.

Paula was all about upscale and nice things. Any time they'd gone on vacation she'd insisted on the nicest amenities.

But she'd wanted to live in the run-down town of Bent, even when they'd had opportunity to move elsewhere. She'd always explained that away as wanting home, but maybe that had been an excuse.

"Maybe I'm going about this all wrong," Will muttered, staring at the water-stained walls of the motel lobby.

"You want to leave?"

"No, not this. I mean maybe I'm going about Paula all wrong. I assumed whoever she was cheating with was someone from our present, but I never thought about her past. She wanted to stay in Bent. When we decided to move here, she said she just loved home. This whole time I've been thinking the affair happened later in our marriage, but…"

It made his stomach roil, but if he could be betrayed later, why not always? "Maybe it was going on all along. Maybe the connection to this guy isn't one I ever knew or even considered, because maybe it's from her life in Bent *before* I came along."

"An ex-boyfriend?" Gracie mused.

"It's possible. I met her in Colorado when she was in college. She was the one who came up with the blacksmith shop idea for me, and suggested I move here. That's when we got married. I didn't know much about her life before that. We didn't dwell on the past, but she wanted to live here. I liked it, too. It was fine with me."

Surely she'd married him because she'd loved him. Surely the affair didn't go back all the way to the beginning of their lives here.

One way or another, he had to find out. Paula was gone. Someone had killed her. Someone was after Gracie and him. He couldn't shy away from the emotional wounds the way he had been doing.

He nodded his chin toward the front desk, where a middle-aged woman in a bright red wig sat, a cigarette dangling from her lips. As the door closed behind them, she made a half-hearted attempt at hiding the cigarette.

"How long you want?" she asked brusquely.

"How long?" Gracie muttered confusedly, further proving to Will just how naive she was.

"How much for a whole night?"

"Big spender, eh?" the woman said with a raspy laugh. "Thirty."

Will went for his pocket before he remembered he had nothing, including no wallet or ID since they hadn't been recovered from his accident.

"Here," Gracie said, sliding two twenties onto the sticky counter. "For tonight and a few hours tomorrow."

"My, my," the woman said with a wink. "Can't say as I blame you." She took the cash, then without getting out of her chair or even looking, reached back and pulled a key off a row of hooks. She put it on the grimy counter and slid it toward them. "Here you go. Get out by noon tomorrow or I'll charge extra."

Gracie looked at the key like it would bite, so Will pocketed it. "Before we go to our room, can I ask you a question?"

The woman eyed him suspiciously. "You know, someone warned me this morning about anybody asking questions."

Will exchanged a surprised look with Gracie. It

had to be connected. Had to be. "What exactly did he say?"

She held up a hand, her nails painted the same red as her wig. She rubbed her thumb against her fingers. "He said a few Benjamin Franklins."

"How many would it take for you to tell us about this warning?"

"I'll be generous since you're easy on the eyes, sweetheart. A thousand."

He didn't particularly want to part with that kind of money, but the bigger issue was accessing it. No ID, no cards.

"I don't suppose I could appeal to your moral compass and have you answer some question about a murdered woman?"

She narrowed her eyes. "What murdered woman?"

"Paula Cooper. She died in a car accident two years ago on the curve of Highway 61 near Bent."

The woman studied Will for quite a few minutes. She even took a drag of her cigarette before she answered. "Car accident. That ain't murder."

"It is if it was caused by someone purposely."

The woman's sharp gaze dropped to his casted arm. "That what happened to you?"

"Someone tampered with my car after I found evidence my wife was killed. I don't consider it a coincidence. If you know something and you're keeping it from me, you can be charged with being an accessory to a murder once they figure this all out." He wasn't sure that was true, but it was a decent enough threat. "Because I will find out who did this. I will make sure the full extent of the law crushes every person who had anything to do with her murder no matter how peripherally."

"Pretty big talk for a man whose dead wife was stepping out on him."

Which he hadn't mentioned. At all. Will's heartbeat picked up. "She came in here, didn't she? With another man?"

The woman shrugged then sighed heavily, dropping her cigarette butt into an overflowing ashtray. "I shouldn't say anything, but I didn't care for those threats I got this morning. I don't know much about much. But I saw the girl who got killed in that car accident quite a few times here with a man and they'd go into a room. But he wasn't the man who came to see me this morning, the man who used to hang around while they did it. I never trusted *that* man."

"Why?"

"Sometimes my daughters work here. Didn't like the way he looked at them. Didn't like the insinuations he made about them in my hearing. Got so bad I stopped scheduling them on Wednesdays because that's when he'd always be here waiting for them. Watching them."

Wednesdays. The computer and the days and Wednesdays. Will leaned across the counter, which had the woman edging back.

"Who is he?" Will demanded.

"Don't know. Just came and skulked around. Guy she came with, don't know him, either. Always paid in cash. Pretty nondescript looking guy. Middle-aged. Hair wasn't brown or blond, somewhere in between. No facial hair, no scars, no tattoos. The watcher, though… Usually all bundled up. Couldn't tell what he looked like, but scary guy."

"What else? Surely if you paid that much attention you know more than that."

She crossed her arms over her chest. "Maybe I do. But any more costs you."

"Look—"

"You come back with a grand and I'll tell you what I know. It might get you what you want."

Will shared a look with Gracie. She shrugged. He fingered the key in his pocket. He hated to walk away, but threatening her wouldn't do any good, clearly. "Thank you. I'll be back with the money." He'd figure out something. He had to.

He strode to the door and once outside, he started for the room number on the key he'd been given.

"What are you doing?" Gracie asked, standing

next to the front office door still. "We need to go get that money."

"How? We can't go back to Bent and I don't have any of my cards anyway. We need to plan first. We'll head to the room and figure something out."

She clearly didn't care for that idea, but she followed him nonetheless.

Chapter Eight

Gracie didn't know how to explain this nervous roil in her gut. Something about being in a room that was clearly not meant for sleeping made her very, very, very uncomfortable.

By the hour.

She knew what that meant, what people did in these kinds of motels. Maybe she was sheltered enough to be a little shocked by such a thing, but she wasn't stupid. At least that's what she was trying to convince herself of.

She was not stupid, and it mattered not at all that Will and her were alone in this room meant for…

She should be thinking about how awful this must be for Will. To stand here and know your wife had come to this seedy, disgusting place only to sleep with another man. And be watched by yet another man. It was too much and too gross.

Gracie wished she had the words to comfort Will,

but he seemed more like a man on a mission again. The old Will, whose entire mind was consumed with Paula's crash.

It was stupid to be disappointed, considering he'd apparently been right this whole time. It was clear he had every reason to be somewhat obsessed with the matter again. They were in danger, and she was a foolish little girl for expecting anything to ever be any different.

"My cousin runs the bank," she said into the quiet of the smelly room. "I could call him, but I have a feeling Cam and Laurel told the whole family not to do anything for me after I stole Cam's truck. Maybe we should have Laurel question that woman. She might be more forthcoming to a police officer."

"I don't know her, Gracie, but I'm gonna guess money is more of a motivator than a county deputy."

He had a point, but she couldn't shake the terrible feeling in her gut. They shouldn't be here. Something was off and wrong.

"So, where can we come up with a thousand dollars? My checkbook is back home, and I only have a twenty left. If we go to the bank or an ATM in Fairmont someone is going to see us and stop us. There's no way Laurel doesn't have the county on the lookout for Cam's truck since I technically stole it."

"A cab. I can take a cab. A twenty could get me to Fairmont, don't you think?"

"Maybe." She sighed, digging her wallet out of her purse. "I've got my credit card if it takes more. I've got enough in my checking account. We should be able to withdraw a grand. We'll just have to use whatever ATM is closest to the highway. Still, it's a safer bet than heading back to Bent."

"You're right. But I think it's safer if I go and you stay here."

"I don't think we should split up." That bad feeling dug in deeper and she hugged herself trying to ward it off. "I don't want to split up."

"I don't want to, either," Will said gently. "But I think it's the safest way. If I get caught, they can't do anything to me. All I did was leave a hospital. You technically stole a truck, and I think they'd use that against you if it meant they could keep an eye on you."

He was right. It sucked, but he was right. Laurel would no doubt throw her in a cell to keep her safe.

"Will—"

But he railroaded right on. "I'll call a cab. Take it to Fairmont. I'll be gone an hour tops and I'll be back with the money and we'll get our answers. We could have this solved by tonight. I'll pay you back as soon as—"

"I don't care about the money. I care about… What if something goes wrong?"

Will turned to her and gently placed his good

hand on her shoulder and squeezed. He looked right into her eyes, certainty and confidence stamped into his expression. "You stay put. The worst thing that happens is your cousins find you and if they do, well, at least you'll be safe."

"When are you going to understand I want you safe, too?" she asked, not sure why her voice came out a whisper or why she thought it would be a good idea to step closer to him.

But he didn't step away, and his hand was still on her shoulder, and for a second she saw a glimpse of what she'd seen in that hospital room. Something different than that laser-beam focus.

But then he shook his head and stepped away, his hand sliding off her shoulder. "We'll both be safe and careful. We have to do this. There isn't another option. This is the first lead we've had. Until Laurel finds something from that text message to you, we have to keep working on our own. I can't wait around. *We* can't wait. We all have to be working toward figuring this out, and like you said in the hospital, we can bend the rules. Maybe with the police department going by the book, and us not, we'll meet in the middle. But we can't stop or wait."

He was right, of course, horrible gut feeling aside. But what was a gut feeling? Wasn't it just worry— and of course she was worried. There was nothing to *not* worry about in this whole situation.

There were no other options. They needed money and they needed to know what that woman knew. Much as Gracie wanted to be skeptical, Gracie had believed the woman's story. She'd known some, and she still knew more. They needed that information.

"Just don't get hurt. Or caught. Or… Just be careful." She swallowed, refusing to give in to the urge to reach out and touch him. She was being overdramatic and so was her gut.

Will called the Fairmont cab company, outlining his plan multiple times while they waited for it to show up. Will stood at the grimy window. "There he is."

He strode for the door, but before he disappeared out of it he stopped and looked back at her. He gave her another one of those weird new looks she wanted to read into, but kept telling herself not to because she was too old to be a mooning idiot.

"Lock the door. Don't open it for anyone. If I'm not back by nightfall, you call Cam or Laurel to pick you up. I don't want you here alone at night. Got it?"

She nodded, but she didn't promise. Because she wasn't about to promise anything if he didn't come back.

WILL SAT LOW in the back of the cab. He had his hood up, trying to obscure as much of his face as possible from the cab driver. He spent the whole drive focusing on Paula and what little he remembered her telling him about her adolescence in Bent.

If he didn't focus on that, he'd focus on Gracie saying *I don't want to split up*, and the way she'd looked at him pleadingly. He'd wanted to give in to that. He'd wanted to give in to too much, and none of it made sense.

Finding Paula's killer was the only sense he could focus on.

Everything in Fairmont went smoothly. The cab took him to the closest bank, waited for him while he walked up to the ATM. He typed in the PIN Gracie had given him and the cash came out without a hitch. Driving back to the hotel, there wasn't so much as a slowdown for wildlife.

Dread pooled in his stomach. He couldn't label this feeling or make sense of it, but it was persistent. Like working on his last ironwork project and knowing it had been all wrong even as he'd gone through all the right steps.

The cab pulled into the lot of the motel and Will scanned the area before he got out. It looked as empty as it had when he'd left. Fat snowflakes were falling from the gray sky and Will struggled to get out of the cab after paying the driver.

He huddled in the oversize coat and trudged toward the room he'd left Gracie in. He had the fleeting thought he should just go talk to the motel lady himself, but with this awful feeling in his gut, he had to make sure Gracie was okay.

She'd been right when she'd said they should stick together. Being apart gave too much room to worry when he had to be thinking and focusing on this whole thing. He wanted to believe Laurel would find something this time, but how could he trust the woman when she and her department had ruled Paula's death an accident?

He knocked on the door, then moved so Gracie would be able to see him out of the peephole, assuming it worked.

She pulled the door open, eyes immediately darting around the lot, as well. "That was quick."

"Everything went just as it should have." He patted his coat pocket. "Let's go talk to her."

She nodded, but he could tell she had that same gut feeling he did. This heavy certainty of impending doom. But there was no way to get rid of that aside from continuing to move forward.

Gracie locked the door and they walked side by side to the front office. It didn't escape his notice they both spent a lot of the time looking around the parking lot as if someone would jump out of the trees or mountains and take them both out.

Gracie stopped short and held her hand out to stop him, too. "Will." She nodded toward the door to the front office.

The window was broken out, when it certainly hadn't been an hour or so ago.

Will swallowed. "Stay here. Call the police."

"No. I call the police and you stay here with me. We can't split up. Everything is all wrong." She pulled her phone out of her pocket and kept her grip on his good arm.

"Don't give them your name. As soon as we make sure she's okay, we're out of here," he murmured as she dialed 911.

She nodded and spoke in low tones to the 911 operator claiming of a break-in at the motel and possible threats and refusing to give her name before she ended the call.

"We have to check to make sure she's okay," Will said. "We can't wait for the cops."

Gracie nodded and they edged forward together. They didn't speak as they moved against the wall of the office. Gracie tried to push forward, but even with the broken arm Will blocked her out, keeping her behind him.

She huffed out an irritated breath, but he ignored it. He glanced back at her when they reached the door, a nonverbal *stay put*.

He wasn't great on reading other people's nonverbal communications, but he was pretty sure the look Gracie gave him was *in your dreams*.

Will used his good arm to reach forward and give

the door a push to see if it would give. When it did, both he and Gracie flinched and froze.

But the door merely squeaked one way, and then clicked back closed. They waited, painfully, to see if someone would come out. If something would happen.

"We have to go in," Will whispered. "She could be hurt."

Gracie nodded soundlessly. So, this time, Will reached out for the knob. He twisted and threw the door completely open. When nothing happened again, he moved into the space of the open door.

Gracie was at his heels, but the room was empty. Completely empty.

"Something's wrong," Gracie whispered.

That's when Will heard a movement and something that could be classified only as a groan. They both hurried toward the front desk, and behind it, sprawled on the floor, was the poor woman from earlier.

They both hopped the desk, kneeling next to the woman. She had a horrible bruise blooming across her cheek and temple, but her eyes fluttered open.

"Ma'am. What happened? What hurts?" Will asked, grabbing her hand. He didn't know how to check for a pulse or what to do in a medical emergency, but it seemed right to give her some kind of human connection.

She groaned again, trying to move, but Gracie urged her to remain still.

"Didn't tell 'em anything," she said, proving she was at least a little with it.

"Here." Gracie grabbed some towels that had maybe once been stacked somewhere but were now scattered across the ground. Will helped her sit up a little and Gracie placed the towels under her head as a makeshift pillow.

"What did they do to you?" he asked.

The woman smiled ruefully then winced. "Tried to beat it out of me. That ain't the way to go about it. You don't lay a hand on me and get what you want. I'll live. Just a little bruised."

She tried to sit up but Gracie wouldn't allow it. "You just lie still till the paramedics get here. You could have a concussion, or something could be broken."

"Don't think so. Well, maybe the concussion. I'm not sure how long they've been gone. Guess I passed out. I'm all right. Let me sit up."

Will helped her into a sitting position and even though she groaned again, she did seem in decent enough shape. It was a relief, and yet someone else had gotten hurt in this whole mess and that wasn't a relief at all.

"Don't know why they left." She furrowed her

brow. "One of them got a call, I think. Or you would've been toast." She smiled ruefully.

"Will," Gracie whispered. "Sirens."

He heard them, too. "Help is almost here. Stay put. Don't move."

"You go on. I'll be just fine. And I won't tell 'em anything. Except about the bastards who tried to hurt me."

"Thank you. Really. Thank you." Will pulled the cash out of his pocket and pulled open the drawer to her desk. "Thank you."

"But I didn't tell you—"

"You were hurt. That's enough. We'll come back if we can." He stood and Gracie stood with him. "We have to get out of here," he said, grabbing her arm and jerking her toward what he hoped to God was a back entrance to the parking lot where the truck was parked.

"He drives a black Ford F250," the woman yelled after them. "The man who was with your wife. Never saw what the watcher drove, but he knew the guy in the truck and your wife, pretty sure. It's not much to go on, but it's something."

"Thank you," Will replied, already pulling Gracie toward the back.

"Where are we going to go?" Gracie demanded, but she followed.

"I don't know." They needed somewhere safe and

off the beaten path. If only whoever was doing this hadn't burned down his cabin. Wait. "You said they burned down my cabin, but what about the shop?" He found the exit to the back lot and pushed through it.

Gracie already had the keys out and jogged toward the truck. "No, no, I think it was fine."

"We'll go there," he said firmly, running to the passenger side.

They both got in and Gracie started the ignition.

"I hope she's okay," she said, pulling forward in the lot.

"She has help now. Real help. Now, we need to figure this out before anyone else gets hurt."

Gracie nodded and pulled out of the parking lot. Through the trees, he could see the flashing lights of a police car pulling off the highway.

"Hurry," he muttered, more to himself than to Gracie.

But she hurried just the same.

Chapter Nine

It was hard to look at the wreckage of the burned-out cabin and not feel both sadness and fury.

"I just don't understand people. How can they hurt all these innocent lives? What do they think they're going to accomplish?"

"Well, getting away with murder would be my guess. Park the truck behind that cluster of trees. It might give us enough of a camouflage that if someone happens up here they won't see it."

Gracie nodded, but she felt beat down. A black Ford F250 was nothing to go on in Wyoming, and what were they going to figure out hiding up here? She should call Laurel. They should let the police handle this. Everything was too dangerous.

Still, she parked the truck in a little grove of trees and about a foot of snow and didn't voice any of her concerns to Will. She was afraid of what his reaction might be.

He was immediately out of the truck, striding through the snow toward his shed of a shop. He didn't even look twice at the wreckage of his cabin, all burned-out boards and collapsed roof.

Gracie couldn't help but look at it. The black jagged remains seemed so grotesque against a fresh inch or so of snow that had fallen only at these higher elevations.

She watched Will stop short at the door of the shed. He, too, was broken and bruised, no matter how fine he walked. That poor woman had been hurt for only the bad luck of working somewhere where people did bad things and would do even worse things to cover it up.

Panic clawed at her chest, but she couldn't give time to it. She followed Will over to the shed, where he stood frowning at the door.

"Someone broke the lock," he said, gesturing toward the hook on the door where a padlock usually kept the door closed if Will wasn't working in it.

"Maybe we should—"

Before she could offer a caution warning, he lifted his leg and kicked the door open. The sight before them made Gracie gasp. His tools were strewn everywhere, many completely broken. Everything had been torn off the walls, ripped or bashed to bits. Even his worktable had been cracked in half.

"Will, I…" But she didn't have the words.

He started forward, picking through the debris. "Well, it should be safe to spend the night here. I doubt anyone will be looking for us in the wreckage." He kicked one of his metal pieces that Gracie couldn't tell if it was a ruined finished piece or just a piece Will himself hadn't finished.

All of this was too much. Even knowing what his reaction would be, she couldn't keep silent. "I should call Laurel."

He turned to face her, that *all about the case* expression on his face. The past two years were coming to a culmination and honestly Gracie didn't know how to deal with that any more than she knew how to deal with the fact these horrible people were out there wanting to hurt them and anyone else who might come into their path.

"If you want to go, Gracie, then I want you to go."

Shocked, she stepped forward. "I'm not *going*. We—"

He shook his head, went back to kicking debris out of the way as if all of this was nothing to him. Just unimportant casualties. "I can't sit back and trust the police. Maybe if anyone had believed me for one second in the past two years I could. I know their weaknesses and I can't wait around hoping that changes."

"I believed you," she said, unaccountably hurt. How many hours had she poured into him? When would she get it through her head? When would she accept this? The only reason he was tolerating her was that she was a means to an end. No matter how many times in the past few days he'd looked at her like she was *Gracie* not the *Angel of Death*. It was an illusion.

"Did you believe me? Or did you just support me?"

"So all that support, all that help, all that *being there*," she said, fisting her hand against her heart so it wouldn't hurt so dang much. "All that only mattered if I believed your story one hundred percent all the time?"

"I was right, wasn't I?"

In all the frustrating times she hadn't been able to get through to him for two long years, she'd never wanted to punch him so much as she did right now. But he was standing there with a broken arm, that horrible blank expression behind his eyes, and even now when he was being such a jerk she wanted to soothe him.

"Like I said, Gracie, if you don't want to be here, then that's what I want for you."

She looked around at the trashed workroom, the broken man in the center of it all. Nothing she felt made any sense. He *had* been right all these years, and didn't he have a right to be a little bent out of shape that no one had believed him?

Except she was helping him and she still felt alone. Separate from whatever was going on in his head. An accessory at best. When she'd risked so much for him, and he couldn't even acknowledge it.

She didn't feel sad anymore. She felt *angry*. Livid. That she was risking life and limb for him, for the truth, and he couldn't even *see* it.

"I helped you when no one else would. I broke you out of the hospital and stole my cousin's truck and gave you a grand to pay off that poor woman. I have cared for you and helped you and all you've done is act like I'm the enemy or a burden or should just leave." Her voice cracked but she couldn't let that stop her. "All you've done is act like this one thing—solving this case—is the only thing in the world that matters." She flung her arms out wide. "It matters, but a million things exist around it. Don't you even care they burned down your cabin? They trashed your shed? You don't even look surprised or hurt or anything. You just want me to leave?"

"I didn't say I wanted you to leave," he replied in that flat, emotionless voice she hated. "I said if you wanted to go, if you want to trust the police, then you should."

"How is that different?" she demanded, something like panic and hysteria winning over every rational voice in her head that told her to calm down and deal with this some other time.

"There is someone after me—"

"Us!" she screeched, and this time she moved toward him, stalked toward him really. He stood his ground, but he looked at her warily and it was *something*. Wary instead of blank. "Someone is after *us*. I am a part of this. That woman back at the motel is a part of this. We're not ghosts you can walk through. We're real-life people putting stuff on the line for the truth. For *you*."

"Can't we have this conversation once we figure out who the hell killed Paula and why? Why would we think about anything else in *this* moment?" He made a gesture around the shed with his good arm. "It's just stuff. But finding out who did this—"

"Won't change the fact that your cabin is gone and your things are broken. It won't change the fact Paula cheated on you, and it doesn't ever change the fact that she's dead. Yeah, you were right, Will. We should absolutely find out who did this. Congratulations. When that's all over, you will have nothing left." She poked him in the chest. "Nothing."

They stood there, facing off, Gracie's breathing too fast and heavy, while he stood there rubbing his chest where she'd poked him.

"What do you want me to do, Gracie?"

"Acknowledge *anything* that is happening. The wreckage, that poor woman, *anything*."

"By doing what? Stopping trying to find the guy?

Cry about my lost stuff or someone getting hurt?
Plan my new, empty life when someone's still after
me? What am I supposed to do? Do some yoga and
breathe? While a killer is out there?"

"You're supposed to look around! Acknowledge
that I have sacrificed for you. That the motel woman,
who doesn't know you from Adam, protected you.
Open your eyes, Will. Just because we're focused
on finding out who did this doesn't mean you can't
acknowledge that life exists around you. That *I* exist
around you."

But he didn't. He stood there with the hint of
a frown turning down his lips. Her words clearly
hadn't penetrated at all, and why was she here? She
could be wrapped up in the Delaney Ranch, safe and
sound with people who loved her taking care of her.

Her best bet was to leave. To work with Laurel
and Cam and try to find the man from the outside.

Because the inside with Will wasn't ever going to
solve anything. It would just be half steps of trying
to stay safe, of Will keeping everything to himself.

If she truly cared about Will, she had to do the
thing that would give him the best chance for being
safe, and she didn't think her being with him was
it anymore.

She stepped away from him, backing away. "If
I'm not your partner in this, if you can't even react
when something like this happens—" she pointed

to the debris "—then there's no reason for me to be here."

With that, she forced herself to turn, to walk toward the door, to not look back. True care wasn't giving someone what they wanted all the time. Sometimes it was doing what needed to be done to protect them.

She was no good to him here, next to him, because all she could focus on was the ways he didn't see her, the ways he didn't see anything and that wouldn't solve the case.

Will had finally gotten his way. The case was all that could matter.

WILL STOOD FROZEN, watching Gracie step out of the shed. He couldn't catch a breath somehow, but this was right. She'd be safer far away from him, and he'd be free to focus on the important things.

The important things were not the wreckage of the cabin that had become his haven. It was not years of work having been destroyed, the debris of it all around him. And it wasn't Gracie's brown eyes wanting something from him.

What could she want from him?

This was the right move. Letting her go. He'd be safe here and he could work through the things he knew. Connect the dots. That motel. A black Ford F250. Paula's past.

Without Gracie.

He was moving forward before he fully realized it. She couldn't go. It wasn't safe for her to go. It was safer if they were together, fighting it their own way without the police. It had to be safer.

He pushed out the door. "Gracie, wait," he called before he realized she hadn't gone very far.

She was standing in the middle of the snowy yard, just staring at the horrible blackened skeleton of his cabin.

He stared at the snow. She wanted him to feel the horrible loss of that, but then how would he ever move again? If he looked around and accepted what he saw, how did any of it matter? How did he not give up?

He forced himself to look up—not at the cabin, but at Gracie. She'd turned to face him and she had tears on her cheeks.

It just about killed him, and again he was moving forward without thinking it through.

"Don't do that. Please don't do that."

She used a hand to wipe one cheek, but before she lifted it to the other, he beat her to the punch, using his fingertips to brush the tears off her cheeks.

Her breath audibly caught, and he didn't know what he was doing, what he was trying to make happen. He didn't understand any of the things happening inside his chest, the jittery feeling of coming to life all over again. The sun was bright and the snow was cold and his cabin and workshop were in ruins and…

And Gracie was here. She'd been through all of it. Holding him up. But it was his turn. His turn.

Awkwardly using his good arm, he managed to pull her to him. Not a hug so much as a lean into each other, because he only had the one movable arm and she didn't reciprocate. He should probably move or something, but she sniffled against his chest and it felt as if the world shifted. Back to being right after being crooked for so long.

Maybe he was delirious.

"I don't want you to go," he murmured against her ear. His nose was somehow buried in her hair and she smelled like flowers and smoke and he was suddenly hit by the fact she'd run into those charred matchsticks of ruin and tried to save his stuff.

"I appreciate that, Will," she said softly, one of her arms tentatively coming around him.

Will couldn't remember the last time he hadn't wanted to be anywhere but where he was, thinking what he was thinking, but everything about Gracie's arm around him was where he wanted to be.

"But maybe it's for the best if I help the police. You don't need me here and—"

He pulled away, trying not to wince as he moved his broken arm all wrong. But he grabbed her upper arm with his good hand and looked her right in the eye. "I do need you here. I absolutely need you."

Her eyes widened, but she didn't say anything to that. She merely stared at him. Eventually she shook her head, that sad determination creeping back into her expression.

He couldn't let her voice those doubts, voice that look in her eye. He couldn't let her keep thinking everything that was all wrong.

"If I open my eyes, if I look around like you want me to, then I have to accept all this is real." The tide of emotions he'd been warding off for two long years threatened to spill right out of him, but Gracie's eyes were his focal point. His reality. He could beat anything off if he could stare at her.

"I would have been lost without you these past two years," he said, something he'd known all this time but had refused to admit to himself let alone out loud. But once he started admitting things, once in this moment of things hurtling out of his control as he almost watched her walk away, it all came spilling out. "Utterly, horribly lost, but if I stared that in its face, then I'd have to accept what a mess I was. That I'd never really dealt with any of the fallout of being cheated on, because instead of divorce or closure, she died. She was *killed*. It's so much easier to want to find the answer to that than deal with the complicated emotions of losing someone you'd loved but didn't anymore. Someone you were so angry with, but didn't deserve to die."

She reached out, her cold fingers brushing against his cheek. In this moment he could admit what he hadn't allowed himself to admit for a very long time. He wanted Gracie to touch him, see him. He wanted *her*, but it was too complicated, too hard and it would mean moving on.

He hadn't been ready to move on. He'd shied away from anything that meant accepting the things he'd felt, dealing with them, and then even scarier, facing new feelings.

"Will, if you accept all these bad things, then you can move forward. Ignoring them means never building a new life." She rested her palm against his jaw and he wanted, more than anything, to stay here. Right here. Answers and murderers be damned.

"Gracie." A new life. For two years that had seemed like the worst possible thing to want or go after. Paula's life was over, and whether he'd loved her still or not, everything about that night felt like it was somehow his fault. His inability to prove someone else had ended her life was his failure.

He didn't deserve a new life, except when Gracie was touching his face, he couldn't help but see it. Want it. Need it.

Chapter Ten

Gracie didn't understand anything that was happening. Most especially the naked emotion on Will's face, which was something she'd surely never seen.

He lifted his good arm and placed his hand over hers on his face. She thought he'd pull it away like he had in the hospital the other day. She'd thought he'd do anything but rest it there, somehow warm against her cold one.

Everything in her chest pulled too tight, and it was hard to breathe. All of this was different, and different was scary. Almost as scary as the situation they were in the middle of.

She should step away from his hand. Step away from him and this. Stick to her guns. But she cared too much, even if it made her stupid.

"We don't need to have this settled to move on," she said gently. "You don't have to have all the answers to plan your life. All the things that happen in a day *are* your life."

"So, crazy murderers after us is my life?"

It wasn't funny, but she found herself smiling. "For today. Yes."

His mouth quirked into that almost smile she used to desperately try to wheedle out of him.

Will's hand moved off her hand, but not to do anything remotely expected. Instead, it slid into her hair, behind her head, and it pulled her closer. She could see a myriad of emotions in his expression. A confusion. A hurt. A warmth she'd occasionally caught sight of before and then convinced herself she was only seeing what she wanted to see.

"Why?" he murmured, and his mouth was so close to hers she could feel his breath. She could see the diamond pattern to that pretty blue of his eyes. She could count the whiskers on his cheek if she wanted to.

There weren't many things she *didn't* want to do when it came to Will. But his question made no sense. "Why what?"

"Two years, I've kept myself shut down. Separate. I haven't been good to you. But even when you gave up on me, you didn't really."

"That isn't true. Well, not fully. You let me help you, and you let me be a part of something that hurt. It might not make any sense to you, but I… Ever since my parents died, even though I bounced around a lot and nobody really wanted me, they all made sure to shelter me. Hadn't I seen enough horrible things? No one ever let me help. No one ever let me be there when something bad was going on."

"Because you were there. In the car with your parents when they died."

She blinked. "How do you know that?"

"You told me. I might not have always admitted to listening, but I was. I was listening." He almost sounded surprised, as though he hadn't realized it himself.

"Well, yes. So, it's not like you were awful to me. You gave me something I'd been searching for. Even if it's a little messed up. It was nice to feel like I was needed, like I could help. You're a good man, Will Cooper. Amidst all this, you were always so *good*."

His fingertips against her scalp pressed harder, bringing her even closer to him. Their bodies brushed and Gracie forgot all about the cold and the people after them. She could only think about his mouth, right there, so close, and somehow he was doing this. Pushing this.

And he wasn't running away.

"I've needed you this whole time," he said, and his lips were so close to hers she could practically feel the words against her mouth. "I don't know anything about being a good man. I know less about moving forward or new lives or living period. Not anymore."

"I could teach you," she whispered, moving onto her toes so she could be that much closer to what she wanted. A new life. Moving forward. It might be the completely wrong time, but how could she not take what she wanted when it was right here? She knew how precarious it all was.

"I think you could," he murmured, and then he closed that last distance, his mouth finally, *finally* meeting hers.

A dream come true that was nothing like her dreams. This was fire and heat and a kind of need that had her shaking at her core. It wasn't sweet or even pretty. It was deeper than all that. Elemental. It had an edge, and if she had any sense to be scared by it, his kiss had obliterated that sense.

"Finally," she murmured against his mouth, making up for the fact he had a broken arm by holding on to him with both of hers.

Not that it mattered. Even with only one good arm, Will held her exactly where he wanted to, his mouth moving against hers as expertly as if they'd done this forever.

She wouldn't mind, but as she shifted against him, he made a little noise, something like an *ouch* he tried to hide in a cough.

She pulled away. "I hurt you."

He shook his head, but it was no use denying it. He was a mess, and she'd forgotten all about it in the haze of that kiss.

Kiss. Amazing, perfect, life-changing kiss. It didn't matter she'd only been kissed a handful of times before. She *knew* this one would change her life.

"I'll live. That's the point, right? Living."

She grinned up at him, feeling some hope in the midst of all this danger. "I like to think so."

He heaved out a sigh and looked around as if he wasn't sure of where they were or how they'd gotten here. She felt the same. Her heart racing, her mouth still tingling.

Will had kissed her. Will. In the middle of all this hell and worry and confusion and danger, and he'd kissed her like she was the center of the universe.

"We're still not safe."

Because they couldn't ignore reality forever, Gracie agreed. "No."

He looked around, and this time when his gaze met the cabin she saw the hurt, the loss. "We should go."

"Go where?"

His eyebrows drew together, but when his gaze returned to hers, there was a determination there that she didn't recognize. It wasn't the blind certainty he'd been following for the past two years. It was different, not that she understood how.

"We're going to your cousin."

She took a step away from him, afraid this was some kind of trick. He was going to make them split up now or— "What? Why would we go to Laurel?"

"We need to find the truth, and I don't know that the police can find it, but maybe you taught me something after all. Doing it alone while they do it alone doesn't solve anything. Maybe we have to work together. We should be safe while we do. So, we go to Cam. We talk to Laurel. They can't bend the rules, no, but four heads are better than one. If there's a new life to be built, we don't risk this one."

We. She might have argued with him, except it was impossible to argue with *we*.

WHILE GRACIE DROVE from the remains of his cabin back down to Bent, Will kept an eye on the road. He couldn't explain what had changed in him up on that mountain, or what had changed in him when he'd pressed his mouth to Gracie's.

But something had changed. Big. Monumental. Or maybe some piece of his old self had finally broken through years of grief.

Was that what that cloud had been? Not just grief that Paula had died, but grief over the dissolution of their marriage. Because this fog, this turning in on

himself and shutting people out had started before
Paula had died.

Then she had died and he'd had something to
blame it all on. Something to drown himself in.

But since that day Gracie had come to his door
with the news Paula had died, she'd been there. This
one lifeline, and in that small connection he'd main-
tained some piece of his old self, no matter how buried.

Now that he realized it, recognized it, had to face
fully the fact that life went on and there *were* new
lives to have, he couldn't possibly risk anyone else in
his single-minded attempt to find Paula's murderer.

There had to be some trust. He might not trust
the Bent County Sheriff's Department, but Gracie
trusted Laurel and Will trusted Gracie. He didn't
know much about Cam Delaney, but Will was somewhat aware he'd been in the military, and that kind of
experience would be helpful in keeping Gracie safe.

In keeping them both safe, from whatever lay
ahead.

In the falling afternoon light, there weren't very
many cars on the road, and Gracie drove them to
the Delaney Ranch. It was a vast, sprawling piece
of land dotted with perfectly kept buildings, except
for one rather ramshackle cabin in the midst of spin-
dly leafless trees in the back. The mountains in the
distance looked like they'd been placed there for a

slow-moving movie landscape shot and everything glittered with ice and snow. Wreaths lined the fences, and bright red bows dotted each north-facing window. Every tree in the sprawling front yard was covered in sparkling white lights shining through early dusk.

"You really grew up here?" Will asked, trying to imagine having this kind of space. This kind of vast freedom.

"Part of the time."

"I don't think I would have left."

She smiled ruefully. "You would have."

He turned to look at her and the little thread of hurt that went along with that statement. She didn't talk about herself much, but when she did, he listened. He knew her parents had died in that car crash with her when she was six. He'd known she'd spent some years in Colorado before moving in with her uncle and cousins here, but he'd never gotten the sense she'd been unhappy. "Why do you say that?"

"My uncle never wanted me here. He was never cruel or mean, but it's tough to be a teenager where you know you're not wanted."

"I think that's tough for any age group."

She stopped in front of the main house, which looked like a sparkling ad for a ranch vacation Christmas. She turned to him, something soft and a little scary on her face.

Because he might have found some old piece of

himself in that kiss, but he still knew he'd grown clumsy with people, with emotions, especially the soft sort.

"I imagine you're right. But I had my cousins, and I have this job that I love. I did all right. I'm doing all right." She pulled a face. "As long as we figure out who's trying to hurt us."

He laughed in spite of himself. "Priorities and all that." But there was something close to vulnerability lurking in Gracie's eyes. He'd never allowed himself to name it before, but that's exactly what it was and he couldn't imagine it stemmed from anything other than a childhood of feeling not particularly wanted.

He could relate to that. He'd forced himself to believe he was different from just about everyone else, but the real reason Gracie had stuck, that he'd allowed her to stick when no one else in his life had these past two years, was a certain kind of understanding.

"You know, it's not like I just *suddenly* noticed I'm attracted to you," he said, because he had a sinking suspicion that was what she'd been telling herself on the drive over.

She raised an eyebrow. "Oh, really?"

He shrugged. "There have been moments."

"What kind of moments?"

He laughed at her straightforwardness. One of the many things he liked about her. Another was that it almost didn't feel odd he was laughing, truly laughing, for the first time in years when they were in the midst of this nightmare.

But something good had been loosed inside him, and he wanted that to last even if someone wanted him dead.

"I think we'll have plenty of time to discuss that later. For right now, let's go inside and face the wrath of your do-gooder cousins."

"There's nothing wrong with being a do-gooder."

"As long as sometimes you acknowledge you have to break the rules."

"Hey, I was the one who stole a truck to break you out of the hospital."

"Yes, Gracie. You are the queen of bad girls."

She rolled her eyes at his sarcasm, but she pulled the keys out of the ignition and pushed her door open. "Time to face the bad girl music."

Will got out of the truck as well and walked with her up the shoveled walk to the front door. It was one of those giant double doors, and the wreaths that adorned both were bigger than Will's head.

Having lived in Bent for not quite a decade he'd understood that the Delaneys ran the show. Gracie's uncle was the mayor and owned the bank, while her cousin ran it. Laurel was a sheriff's deputy, and another Delaney sibling ran the general store. The Delaney name was splashed over everything. He'd understood they were a big part of the town, but he hadn't fully taken that on board until he'd stood right here in the front of this sprawling house in the midst of this picture-perfect ranch.

Gracie knocked on the door. He didn't know why that struck him as odd. He'd certainly never bust into his mother's house without knocking, but Gracie was, well… She was far different. He was surprised she didn't belong just everywhere.

When the door opened, it was neither Laurel nor Cam, but Geoff Delaney. Gracie's uncle. Mayor of Bent. A man who looked quite unhappy to see his niece.

"Well, well, well," Mr. Delaney said, crossing his arms over his chest. He was a neat, well-put-together older man. But there was absolutely no warmth in him as he gave Gracie a disapproving look. "You've been causing quite the commotion, Grace."

"Hi. I'm sorry. If Cam is still looking for me—"

"You stole his truck. Of course he's looking for you. Half the town is looking for you. What you've done is very inconsiderate and childish. Instead of coming inside, I suggest you head down to the police station and turn yourself in."

"Surely that's not necessary," Will said, the words out of his mouth before he had the sense to keep his mouth shut and his nose out of her family business.

"No. He's right. We'll go. I'm sure we can get a hold of Laurel there."

Will couldn't believe what he was witnessing. As much as he didn't get along with his mother and even less with his stepfather, they wouldn't have treated him like a criminal. They'd be ambivalent, sure, but not cold and dismissive. Besides, he'd deserved their censure. He'd been a surly ass of a teenager.

He couldn't imagine Gracie being anything but sweet and kind. Giving. Someone treating her casually cruelly didn't add up. At all. "You'd think family would want to help their own," Will said, glaring at Mr. Delaney.

Gracie pulled on Will's good arm, trying to get him off the porch. "It's not important. Let's go find Laurel and—"

"*I* would think a stranger would mind his own business," Mr. Delaney said, his voice harsh and even darker than it had been when talking to Gracie.

There was something about that voice that Will couldn't quite place or put together, but it gave him a strange chill. So he let himself be pulled back to Cam's truck by Gracie.

They got back into the truck and no matter that Gracie tried to put on a brave face, Will could tell she'd been upset by that whole interaction.

He was bothered by it, too, and not just the way

her uncle had treated her with such coldness. Something about Mr. Delaney's voice was weirdly familiar. The kind of familiar that made him edgy, suspicious.

His eyes caught the giant four-car garage as Gracie turned the truck around and headed back out to the highway.

"Gracie, this is going to sound very, very strange, but what kind of car does your uncle drive?"

"Oh, one of those giant Ford…" Her head whipped toward him before she looked back at the road. She began shaking her head. "No. That's… No."

"He drives a black Ford F250."

"I could name ten people from Bent who have black Ford F250s. We don't even have a year on it. My uncle is… Will, no."

"It's an awfully strange coincidence."

"But it is a coincidence. It's impossible my uncle had anything to do with this. He prides himself on being moral and good and the mayor of the town. He would never kill someone."

"He wasn't very nice to you."

"There's a big difference between not nice and cold-blooded killer. Honestly, if he wanted to murder people, I think the Carsons would have been wiped out years ago. It's a weird coincidence, sure, but I'm not sure why you would make that jump. It's a big jump."

"Something about his voice was familiar." Will wished he could place it, understand it. "Something about this is all messed up. I think we need to look into your uncle."

Chapter Eleven

It was impossible. It was insane. But as she drove Cam's truck toward the police station, Gracie couldn't help but try to connect the very confusing dots.

"My uncle would have been like twenty years older than your wife at least."

"Gracie, don't be naive."

Gracie scowled. "What? That's gross."

"Plenty of women have relationships with older men. Much older men. We're not exactly close in age, and you did kiss me."

She gave him a doleful look. "You are eight years older. Not an entire lifetime." She shook her head, turning onto the road that would take them around Bent toward the Bent County Police Station. The route down Main Street would be quicker, but this way they might be able to avoid detection till they got to Laurel themselves. "I just can't imagine my uncle being wrapped up in any of this. I can't."

"Maybe you're right. Maybe this is all coincidence. But I can't ignore a coincidence just because you're related to it."

He was right. Objectively she understood he was right. But she knew Uncle Geoff. He wasn't the nicest guy, but a murderer? It didn't add up.

"If we tell Laurel about what happened at the motel—"

"We cannot tell Laurel about this coincidence. This is her *father*. I wouldn't say she idolizes him, but she certainly respects him and loves him. You can't ask his kids to look into him being a killer."

Will nodded, and Gracie tried to concentrate on her driving, but her gaze kept moving back to Will.

"We need to talk to a Carson," he finally said.

Gracie wrinkled her nose. "Why would we talk to a Carson?"

"Paula was a Carson. She wanted to live in her hometown. I didn't really have one of those, so I didn't question it. It sounded nice, to have a hometown."

"It is."

"But she wasn't close with her parents. I wasn't either, so I didn't question that, either. But if we put those things together—hometown but not being close with your family."

"I hate to break it to you, but I love Bent and my uncle isn't my favorite person."

"Yeah. Yeah, but I spent two years looking into Paula's present. Her job, the people she worked with. Her friends. I never went back to before we met because that didn't make sense. But she wanted Bent even though she could have had a better job elsewhere. She wanted Bent even though she wasn't particularly close with her parents. Maybe it's nothing, but a Carson might be able to tell me that."

"Okay. Which Carson? I have to warn you though, I'm not sure how far we're going to get in a basically stolen truck, or with a Carson for that matter."

"She'd go drinking with a group of second cousins sometimes. One was in the army or something and they'd get together when he was on leave. I'm not sure I ever met him since he wasn't around much. Ty, I think. Ty Carson. You know where he lives?"

"Yes, but Ty Carson is Grady Carson's cousin. Grady Carson is engaged to Laurel. And they all live together either on their ranch or in Rightful Claim."

"Jeez. Small-town life is no joke. Okay. Well, we'll try to find Ty. Ask him about Paula. Her parents never believed me regarding the affair, and they'd lost their daughter so I never pushed there. But the second cousins were more friends. Maybe she said *something*." He frowned, but kept barreling forward. "We'll talk to Ty about people in Bent Paula might have had a history with. Maybe he doesn't know about an affair, but maybe he says something that clicks. We won't mention your uncle or anything else. We'll focus on the past. If it doesn't lead us anywhere, and Cam and Laurel don't find us first, we'll make our next choice from there."

"Okay, we can try the Carson Ranch first. If Ty's not there, Noah might know where he is. But I have to warn you, Grady and Laurel might be engaged but that doesn't mean Carsons love Delaneys. Particularly Delaneys who deal in death."

"I'll admit, I never paid much attention to Paula when she was ranting about the feud. Because I think a century-old feud is ridiculous, but I never got the sense one side was evil."

"You must not have been listening hard enough."

Will smiled a little at that. "What I mean is it sounded like a bunch of misunderstandings and blame. Sure some of the ancestors along the way were jerks, but it always sounded like a bunch of people trying to do the right thing—and just not agreeing on what the right thing is."

"And by 'not agreeing' you mean 'feuding bitterly over it.'"

Will shook his head, but Gracie supposed he wasn't wrong. Except for the people who were after them who definitely didn't want the right thing, all the Carsons and Delaneys she knew were mostly good, mostly trying to do the right thing. Maybe not so much in the past, but now.

All her interactions with Ty and Noah and Grady over the past few months since Grady had gotten involved with Laurel hadn't just been civil—there was a kindness there, too. She had to admit that they weren't the odious, evil caricatures the Delaney side often made them out to be. Most especially her uncle.

"You don't think it could all connect to the feud, do you?" Will mused.

Gracie wanted to immediately deny it, but the fact of the matter was the people she knew who took the feud the most seriously were her uncle and Jesse Carson, who'd been in jail for the past two years. "How was Paula related to Jesse Carson?"

"Max and Jane Carson are her parents."

"If I have my family trees correct, I think Max is Jesse's brother. That would make him Paula's uncle. Sound right?"

"I think so. What does Jesse have to do with any of this? I'm not sure I've ever even met him."

"He's in and out of jail, so it doesn't surprise me you might not have had any family gatherings with him. But I was just thinking about the people who take the feud the most seriously, as in would possibly cause physical harm to someone from the other side."

"And you came up with Jesse Carson? She definitely wasn't having an affair with her uncle."

"No, but I was thinking about Jesse Carson and *my* uncle. They take the feud very seriously." Gracie didn't have to look at Will to know he was giving her a lifted eyebrow, *but you don't think your uncle is a murderer* look.

And she didn't, but that didn't mean there wasn't some more complicated connection here. She couldn't rule anything out. Just like when she was examining a body, she couldn't let her assumptions or presumptions rule her findings. She had to let the evidence speak for itself.

Somehow they made it all the way around Bent to the other side where the Carson Ranch spread out as if it was in an Old West standoff with the Delaney Ranch on the exact opposite side of town. Facing each other. Always ready to fight.

But where the Delaney Ranch was all polish and sparkle, the fence in front of the Carson Ranch was run-down and old. Gracie took the turn onto the gravel road that led them up the hill to the main house.

"I guess it's possible that Cam and Laurel gave up and went back to their own lives instead of trying to find us," she offered.

"Judging from the red and blue lights flashing behind us and a very angry man marching at us from the tree line, I don't think so."

Gracie flicked a glance in her rearview mirror, and sure enough a Bent County Sheriff's Department cruiser was behind them. When she looked to the tree line, Cam was marching toward them on foot.

Gracie offered Will a somewhat sheepish shrug. "I guess we won't be talking to any Carsons."

"We could always make a run for it."

Gracie laughed as Cam stormed toward them. "I know for sure that I cannot outrun a marine, and maybe you could if you weren't broken and bruised. But you are."

He made a scoffing noise. "I'm not *that* broken."

"Then why are you still sitting here? Make your run for it," she challenged.

He reached out, surprising her by gently touching a stray strand of hair and tucking it behind her ear. He looked at her, his expression not exactly grave, but certainly not cheerful. "We're in this together. No matter what. Deal?"

She inhaled and smiled at him, because Will had kissed her. Will had wanted to come back and be safe. They were in this together. "Deal," she returned, more hopeful than she'd been in days.

WILL STEPPED OUT of the truck at the same time Gracie did. Both Delaneys barreled toward them, even as Will and Gracie stood still.

When they approached, there was nonstop yelling and demands, though Will couldn't make out any of it since Cam and Laurel were yelling and demanding over each other.

Gracie held up her hands, giving them both quieting looks. "I know you're both angry."

The two started shouting again, but Gracie waited them out. Patient. Strong. She had such a presence about her, and for the first time in two years Will wanted to get beyond this case, beyond the truth, and really figure out that *what then* on the other side.

"I'm sorry," Gracie said, sincerity all over her face. "I know you think I was in the wrong, but I did what I had to do."

"You could have been killed," Cam and Laurel said in unison. Then they both gave Will almost identical murderous looks.

"We thought we'd be better off trying to figure this out alone, but we both realized we were wrong. We actually went by the Delaney Ranch to talk to you, but you weren't there, so we started talking. Will has some theories."

Laurel started. "Will can shove his theories up his—"

Cam cut off Laurel. "Easy," he muttered, calming his sister down. "What kind of ideas?"

"I never really looked into Paula's life before we met. I assumed whoever she was having an affair with, whoever would have killed her, it would have been someone in her life since us moving to Bent."

"We still don't have evidence Paula was killed, Will." Laurel shook her head. "I'm sorry, but—"

"*I'm* sorry," Will interrupted. "But I do believe that's what happened, and as long as Gracie's in danger, that's the lead I'm going to follow. Paula was a Carson. I know she used to go drinking sometimes with Ty Carson. I wanted to talk to him."

"Ty has spent most of the past ten years in the army," Laurel replied.

"But not all. He'd come home for leave and spend some time with Paula. Him and some other second cousin I can't remember. But I know they did, and Paula would always tell me not to bother to come with. It was 'family time.' So, maybe she talked to Ty or something, or maybe they just know something about an ex or relationship before I came along that might give us a lead."

"Is it smart to focus on the murder and cheating as one thing?" Laurel asked, and Gracie appreciated that there was an amount of gentleness in her voice that hadn't been there before.

"I don't have any other angles, and…" He flicked a glance at Gracie and she stepped forward.

"We found a motel Paula used to go to. We talked to the woman who ran the motel and she told us—"

Laurel swore. "You better not mean the Tick Tock Motel between here and Fairmont." When Gracie only smiled sheepishly, Laurel swore again. "You are *killing* me, Gracie."

"Listen. She told us Paula used to go in there with a man. And another man used to watch them. She told us the kind of car the man who was with Paula drove."

"And got her skull bashed in the process," Laurel added, glaring at Will.

"I'm sorry she got hurt," Will said. "I take responsibility for it, I do. I wasn't thinking beyond finding the truth, and I'm trying to take more care, but until this man is caught, anyone could be hurt."

That seemed to cut through at least a little bit of Laurel's irritation, if possibly none of Cam's military blankness.

"Did you find anything about Will's phone?"

Laurel shook her head. "No. Whoever used it to text you has it turned off, so it's not traceable." Laurel eyed Gracie then Will. "I'll take you up to the house. If Ty isn't there, someone will know where he is. But if we're working together it means I need to know everything, and it means we need to be able to trust each other. You can't run off again."

"Of course not," Gracie said gently. But Laurel wasn't looking at Gracie, she was scowling at Will.

He was tempted to stare her down, or maybe promise Gracie wouldn't run off again. Laurel didn't have any say over him. But Gracie was looking at him expectantly, with just enough concern in the set of her eyebrows to have him giving in.

"We won't run off," he promised.

"You know what will help with that?" Cam asked, his voice alarmingly casual. "Giving me my truck back."

Gracie winced, but she dug out Cam's keys and handed them to him. "I am sorry. It was the only option."

Cam raised one eyebrow, very slowly. Quite the trick.

"Okay, maybe it wasn't the only option, but it was... Well, I'm sorry."

Cam nodded, pocketing the keys. "And you two are under my protection until further notice, which means I'll follow you."

Will chafed at the idea of someone "protecting" him, but surely what Cam meant was Gracie. Will could pretend he needed protection for Gracie's sake.

Unfortunately there was one thing he couldn't do for Gracie's sake. "There is something we found out that you should both know about."

Gracie squeezed her eyes shut in dismay, but she had to know this was information they needed to share. "The woman at the motel told us the man my late wife was having an affair with drove a black Ford F250."

"I guess that's *something*," Laurel said. "But it

was a few years ago. It doesn't mean whoever it is still drives that, or that this necessarily connects."

"But it's something to go on." He almost opened his mouth to remind Laurel her father drove that kind of truck, but Gracie's gaze was pleading.

Well, clearly he wasn't going to get anywhere with convincing a man's family members he was a liar, cheater and possibly murderer.

But that didn't mean it wasn't the theory he'd be working to prove.

Chapter Twelve

Gracie couldn't blame Noah Carson's greeting scowl when three Delaneys showed up on his porch. One even in uniform.

"No one's dead, are they?" he asked, glaring in Gracie's direction.

"Not today." She managed a wan smile. "Things have been very quiet. Unusual for this time of year."

He rolled his eyes before the sound of a young boy shouting *no* started emanating from the house. A pudgy little toddler appeared on his hands and knees before sitting back on his diaper and lifting his arms. "No!"

Noah scowled at them, but when he bent down to pick up the boy everything about him softened. "Well, I guess you want to come in," he grumbled, moving out of the doorway.

Laurel and Cam went first, which irritated Gracie a little. She wanted to be running this show because she knew more. She knew Laurel had worked hard on the case of Paula's accident, but Gracie had an intimate acquaintance with it. Two years' worth of going over it with Will.

But they were all working together now, and Gracie had to let some things go. Laurel was the cop. The one who'd have to actually build a legal case against whoever they found guilty.

Please, God, let us find the guilty party.

"Is Ty here?" Laurel asked.

Noah narrowed his eyes as he settled the baby in a high chair. "What do you want with Ty?"

The front door swung open and Addie Foster, arms heavy with bags, stepped inside already talking.

"Sorry I'm late. I was talking to Jen and… This is a lot of Delaneys in our kitchen. Did someone die?"

Addie might be newer to Bent than the rest of them, and her Delaney relation was far down the line, but she'd certainly picked up on the history quickly since moving here to become Noah's maid earlier in the year. Of course, based on the kiss they shared as Addie transferred the bags to Noah, and Noah's carefulness with Addie's baby, Gracie had to assume things had gotten rather personal.

"No one's dead," Gracie said almost simultaneously with Laurel.

"Ty's in trouble," Noah said.

"No," Laurel corrected. "We need to talk to him.

There isn't any trouble. It's about someone he used to know."

"This seems very ominous," Addie said, eyebrows drawing together in concern.

"The case I'm working on is serious, but Ty hasn't got anything to do with it. He just had contact with someone and we want to talk to him about anything he might have heard."

"So, what's with the posse?" Noah demanded.

Laurel crossed her arms over her chest and stared Noah down. "Are you going to tell me where Ty is or do I have to text Grady?"

Noah grunted. "Stables."

"Thank you," Laurel said. She patted the baby on the head as she moved back for the door.

"Couldn't you give us a clue as to what's going on?" Addie asked as the group followed Laurel back to the front door.

"Sorry, Addie. It's fairly unconnected though, and hoping Ty might remember a conversation from a few years ago is a pretty big leap."

"What confidence," Will muttered, and Gracie nudged him disapprovingly.

They filed out the door and since Laurel knew her way around the Carson Ranch, they all followed her, trudging through the snow to a large building that was clearly the stables.

When they reached the building, Laurel walked

right in. In the tradition of all the Carsons, Ty was a large, intimidating-looking man and the glare he sent Laurel had Gracie taking a few steps backward.

Of course, that only knocked her into Will, who let out an *oof* when she jarred his broken arm.

Ty studied them all with a kind of calm that reminded Gracie of Cam. Ty had been in the military, too. There was a stillness to it, but there was a sense that he was ready to strike at any moment that put Gracie a little bit on edge.

"This feels like an ambush, Delaney. Or should I say Delaneys." He tilted his head. "Plus that guy." He squinted. "I know you."

Will rocked back on his heels. "Will Cooper. I was married to Paula."

"Paula." He sighed. "A shame about Paula."

"Something has recently happened that leads us to believe—"

Ty held up a hand, and Gracie was shocked to watch Laurel snap her mouth shut. She was clearly irritated, but she quieted nonetheless.

"Are you here on official business, Deputy?"

Laurel pulled a face. "Sort of."

"Sort of?"

"Ty—"

"No. You talk," he said, pointing at Will.

"You're such a caveman," Laurel muttered, but she turned to Will and gave him a little nod as if to give him the go-ahead.

Will cleared his throat. "Ah, well, I haven't ever thought Paula's death was an accident."

"Pretty common knowledge."

"Right, well, it looks like I might have been right." Ty looked to Laurel. "Officially, right?"

"Possibly."

"Hell. But what's it all got to do with me?"

"You knew Paula," Will said firmly. "You were friendly with her. Maybe you knew, if not who she was having an affair with, someone who might have known something. A mention of someone that seemed off. Something."

"That was years ago, man. And only when I was on leave. I don't know…"

"It's a long shot, but if you think of anything, I'd appreciate—"

"Bent County Sheriff's Department would appreciate the information," Laurel finished for Will.

Ty rubbed a hand over his beard. "I don't know. But Kayleigh might. Kayleigh Gentry. I don't know how close they were at the end there, but they were really good friends as kids. The three of us would always get a drink when I was in town."

The twisted web of feud nonsense just got more complicated. "Kayleigh is Jesse Carson's daughter," Gracie murmured gravely.

Ty nodded at Gracie. "Yeah."

She shared a look with Will. She'd thought any

connection to the feud had to be a reach when Will had first suggested it, but now she wasn't so sure.

"If I think of anything else I'll let you know," Ty said, nodding toward Will.

"You'll let *me* know," Laurel said firmly.

Ty flashed a grin and gave her a little shrug. "Guess we'll see."

Laurel grunted and whirled on a heel to leave the stables, Cam, Will and Gracie following. Once they were outside the stables, heading toward their vehicles, Laurel whirled on Will.

"If he says *anything* to you, I want your word you'll immediately share it with the police."

"We came here to work with you guys. That's what we're going to do."

Laurel didn't exactly seem thrilled with that answer, and Gracie had to admit it filled her with a certain kind of trepidation considering Will hadn't given his word at all. But Laurel marched for her cruiser, and Gracie followed at the same slow speed Will did.

"You're not lying, are you?" Gracie said in a low voice she hoped Laurel couldn't hear.

Will gave her an enigmatic look, then simply shrugged.

WILL HAD NO desire to be cooped up at the Delaney Ranch, no matter how comfortable it was, but both

Cam and Laurel had insisted they spend the night there. Gracie hadn't put up a fight, either.

He wanted to hunt down Kayleigh Gentry, not wait around for Laurel to decide when it was appropriate. Not spend the night in the same house as Gracie's uncle.

"I thought we'd be working *with* them, not be their prisoners," he grumbled as Gracie showed him to his room.

Gracie laughed, a pretty, bright sound as she pushed open a door. It seemed every room in this monstrosity of a house was magazine perfect and decorated for Christmas.

"I probably should have warned you neither Laurel nor Cam are very good at compromise. But you're in luck."

"I am?" He tried to focus on what she was about to say, but there was a very big bed in the middle of the room, and as much as they'd traveled here, there and everywhere all day, he hadn't been able to put that kiss out of his mind. Every time he looked at her, he could only think to that one perfect moment where he'd felt her mouth under his, where he'd suddenly, glaringly remembered that there were things in the real world that were worth engaging in.

"I may have a few get-around-Laurel tricks up my sleeve," she continued, clearly clueless to what he was thinking about.

She looked so pleased with herself and they were finally really alone for the first time since their drive to Bent and—

And on the chase for a potential murderer, that she might not believe was the man who owned this house, but Will had some suspicions.

But she looked so happy, and he'd forgotten that happy could be a thing. For years he'd existed in something else and the more he'd isolated himself, both before and after Paula's death, the less there'd been any of this. He hadn't realized he'd missed it till it was here, gorgeous and irresistible right in front of him.

"Why are you looking at me like that?" she asked, smoothing an almost shaky hand over her hair.

"Like what?"

"I don't know." She wrinkled her nose. "Usually it's more like looking through me, but that's... I..."

"I never looked through you." No, she'd always been twin sides of a coin existing in one person. A lightness he'd wanted but had been afraid to look too hard at. "I purposefully ignored you."

"Why?"

"I've been in a bad place for a lot of years."

"You were getting better, you know," she interrupted, stepping toward him, always ready to go to bat for him. "Maybe not with the whole going-to-

town thing, but your art pieces, getting back into that, was a big step and—"

"You don't need to defend me to me, Gracie. You're right. Something was changing and I tried to shy away from that, too, but you were always there. You've been the…" He was crap at words. Always had been. Even knowing she deserved them, he really couldn't come up with anything.

So he closed the small distance between them and reached out to touch her cheek. Unlike that kiss from this afternoon that had exploded out of nowhere, he took his time. To feel the soft texture of her cheek, to move closer inch by inch and actually watch the pinkish color rise to her cheeks.

He let himself forget everything and just exist in this moment. There was something so completely life changing in breathing this in, letting things go, and giving in to everything that Gracie had ever been to him these past few years.

But before he actually got the chance to sink into all that, someone knocked on the door.

Gracie squeezed her eyes shut, a soft groan escaping her mouth. "Oh, right." She stepped away and gave her head a little shake. "Jen. Jen knows Kayleigh and was going to get me her number. So, that's…"

"Jen," he finished for her, finding some amusement in how flustered she seemed. He'd been such a mess for years, flustering anyone felt like a kind of power.

"Yes. My cousin Jen."

"Jeez, how many cousins do you have?"

"Oh, lots. Lots. Delaneys never leave for long. I should answer the door. I should answer it," she stuttered.

"You might want to stop blushing."

She opened her mouth, something like outrage threading through her features. "You know you have absolutely no room to poke fun at me, Mr. Hermit."

He grinned. "That so?"

She made a little huffing noise then moved to her tiptoes and in a smooth move she pressed her mouth to his, quick and not nearly enough, before giving him a sassy little look. "That's so," she muttered, walking to the door.

She opened it for yet another Delaney. Will tried not to sigh. It was a strange change in his life to finally want to be done with this. He didn't want the puzzle anymore. He wanted after the puzzle.

"So, I got you that phone number," Jen said, handing Gracie a sheet of paper. Then she turned and smiled at him. "Hi, Will."

"Jen." He vaguely knew her as the woman who ran the Delaney General Store, though he wasn't sure why he'd never put together she was also Gracie's cousin. There were just too many people in that damn family to keep track of.

"How much is Laurel going to hate me for letting you have this?" she asked, smiling at Gracie.

"Depends on what we get out of it."

Jen grinned at that. "Noted. Well, I'll let you two get to it. I know it's late, but if you want some dinner, I left some chili in the Crock-Pot for Dad."

"Is it just going to be us and him tonight?"

Jen pulled a face. "Cam will be around, but he's out front working on some kind of video monitor to put at the entrance." Jen rolled her eyes. "You want me to stay and play buffer?"

"No, no. Don't go through any trouble on my account."

"It's not any trouble. I can talk spreadsheets and profit margins with Dad and give him the thrill of his Saturday night. I'll keep him in his office so you don't have to deal if you want to go eat." Jen patted her pocket. "I've got my phone on me, so text if you need something you don't want to risk running into Dad for." She squeezed Gracie's arm, then gave Will a wink and disappeared out the door.

Gracie looked down at the paper in her hand. "So, do you want to call her, or should I?"

Will stared at the paper, too. Thought about Laurel wanting to work together. Thought about all Gracie had done for him these past two years. The fact she was staying here in this place that made her uncomfortable and avoiding her uncle, all for him, when he hadn't done a thing in two years to deserve it.

But she'd seen beneath the bitterness and the shell. She'd been the support he'd needed to pull himself out of something dark, and in this moment he didn't care about the case, about murderers or his broken arm or Paula's death.

"I think we should wait."

Chapter Thirteen

"Wait? Wait for what?" Gracie asked. He was staring at her so intently and she didn't get it. They had a lead and he wanted to wait? This was not the Will Cooper she knew. Oh. His injuries. "Is your arm bothering you? Did you want some ibuprofen? Maybe some sleep would—"

"No."

He touched her cheek again, just as he had before Jen had knocked. As though he was touching something beautiful and precious and Gracie hadn't a clue what to do with *that*. Yes, she'd had an unfortunate crush on Will for most of the past two years so there'd been a certain level of fantasy about him touching her, kissing her.

But somehow all those silly fantasies didn't match *this*. She didn't have people in her life who looked at her like she was a marvel, who touched her like she was precious. She had protectors in Laurel and

Jen and Cam, but no one had ever focused on her exactly like this.

"Gracie, I want to start living my life." He said it so earnestly, and still those blue eyes were focused on her. Not through her, not on anything else but her. Will Cooper was staring at her like she was the center of his world.

It wasn't about the case, or his dead wife or anything else. That might be why they were here, but that wasn't why he was talking about his life. *She* was why he was talking about living. *She'd* gotten that out of him.

"I want that, too. For you. You have a lot of life left to live, and I think you'd be good at it if you gave it a shot."

He laughed, a low rumble of a chuckle that drifted across her temple. "What on earth from the past two years makes you think I'd be any good at it?"

She looked up at him, trying to speak past the way his fingers drifting down her neck backed up the breath in her lungs. "You're good at going after the truth, and you make beautiful things out of metal. You could make beautiful things out of life, you just have to want to."

He kissed her then, and she couldn't understand how it could be softer, sweeter, while still filling her with all the same things she'd felt up on the mountain earlier. Fire and heat and need. There was a sharpness to it all, no matter how gentle he was. The jagged, painful rightness of finding a new beginning in the midst of something bleak and ugly.

His good arm held her tight against the hard length of his body, and his mouth explored hers with a kind of studied leisure that had warmth pooling through her. Her knees felt weak—her heart felt too big for her chest.

Though it was gentle to begin with, everything softened second by second. Well, except him. His body seemed harder and harder and more this pillar of stone and strength and she wanted all of that more than she'd ever wanted anything.

She raked her fingers through his hair. She arched against him, chasing this edgy, desperate need she'd never felt with anyone else. Not like this. It had always been Will. The one man she'd ever wanted to give herself to.

There was a bed. There was time. She could finally have this thing she wanted and nothing else had to matter. Nothing else. Just for a little while.

"Gracie?"

She didn't know what he was asking, but it didn't matter. "Yes."

Then heat didn't begin to describe what exploded between them. It was so much more, so much bigger than anything. He kissed her everywhere and she slid her hands under his shirt, taking care to be gentle against his broken arm—the hard cast the only reminder he was even hurt at all.

His hand slid over her breast, and even through the fabric of her shirt and bra, he found her nipple with his thumb, brushing against it even as he kissed her mouth, with something like *hunger*.

"I'd take off your shirt but I'm sadly one-armed these days, so you're going to have to help me with the whole clothing removal."

She had her shirt off in seconds, no matter how her heart jittered. "Now let me help you."

He sat on the edge of the bed and she moved to stand in between his legs as she carefully peeled the shirt off him without jarring his broken arm.

She let the shirt fall, standing in between his legs as he looked the short distance up at her small frame. He looked at her like she was a gift or a prize or something wonderful and for one horrible second she was so afraid. Because it didn't make any sense that anyone could look at her that way.

"Are you sure… Are you sure I'm not just convenient?" she whispered.

He laughed, a full-on grin she'd never seen on him as he curled his hand around her hip and drew her even closer. "Oh, sweetheart, I'm not sure anything about you is *convenient*. Convenient would be spending the rest of my life holed up in a cabin ignoring the world. *Convenient* would be letting whoever is after me finish the job."

"Don't say that!"

"I'm just saying there isn't anything about wanting to get back out there that's easy or convenient, but it's what I want. *You're* what I want. A life with you in it. A real one, too, not one centered on a mystery or the past."

"I used to think I should say something, or let you know that I… I mean, I've…"

"You're attracted to me."

She had no idea why that cocky glint to his blue eyes made her feel that much more like Jell-O but it did.

"God knows why," he muttered.

It was that hint of bafflement that soothed some of those nerves, some of that insecurity. "I'm attracted to you and I *like* you, Will. Because even at your worst, you're a good man. But you weren't ready to hear any of those things."

"No, I wasn't."

She cleared her throat, trying to focus on what she wanted to say more than the nerves fluttering around in her stomach. "Are you ready now?"

"To know you think I'm a good man, no. To try to be that man, yes. To act on this attraction, hell yes. Part of me thinks we should figure everything out first. Who might have tried to hurt us both. It's such a big, all-encompassing thing. But my life for the past two years has been trying to figure it out. Shutting everyone and everything down until my life was only finding out who did this. We're so close to something, when I haven't been close to anything in years."

Her hope and giddiness sank a little. "Right."

"But you were right back there at the wreckage of my cabin. It's all life. Finding it out. Exploring this thing with you. You don't know what kind of time you have. You don't know what's going to happen or not, and if you're not moving forward toward the things you want, you're likely to never get it."

She threaded her fingers through his hair, holding his head at an angle that kept his gaze on hers. "What do you want? I mean specifically out of life?"

"I'm not sure quite yet. I like what I do metal-working wise, so more of that. And I like you. I want more of *you*." He drew her as close as he could stand to him. "What do you want?"

She blinked at him, trying to reconcile a million things, most of all that he was asking what she wanted and waiting for an answer.

"Don't you know?" he asked, cocking his head.

"Yes, *I* know, but you've never stopped to wonder what I want before. I'm still getting used to this new you."

His mouth quirked—more and more, she was getting that reaction out of him. "Just because I didn't ask didn't mean I didn't wonder. This me isn't new. It's just been hidden under a lot of ugly things. You're the only thing I've wanted to crawl out of it for."

She sucked in a breath.

"I'm probably a bad bet," he murmured.

She leaned down, smiling. "I'll take it anyway," she offered before pressing her mouth to his.

WILL CURSED HIS broken arm. He could deal with not having both hands to peel off her pants. Watching her shimmy out of them, or help him with his, well, no one could complain about that. Naked except for her underwear, she was gorgeous. And even though the pale hue of her skin gave an aura of delicateness to her, the strength of all Gracie was emanated from those dark eyes, all certainty and heat.

He wanted to be on top of her—he wanted to be able to move. He wanted this moment in time to be the best, most explosive thing she'd ever experienced.

And he had one functional arm and a million bruises to ignore. He only had one hand to touch her. One hand to use to explore the gorgeous curve of her breast, the soft, sumptuous skin of every part of her. The way her skin was as soft as velvet, but the muscles under all that skin were the truth of her.

Of course, he also had a mouth. He used both as best he could, until she was panting, saying his name like a prayer. Until he was so hard it hurt and all he could think about was losing himself in everything Gracie had always been to him.

He managed to sprawl out and maneuver her on top of him, though he had to hide a wince at the tinge of pain that went through his broken arm. "You're going have to help me out here," he managed to grind out. But it wasn't the pain of his arm that had his voice scraping against the sweet, heavy *need* of the room. It was clawing frustration thinking he couldn't give her everything she needed.

"Oh. *Oh*." She blinked, looking down at her hands splayed over his chest as if she hadn't quite realized how she'd gotten here. "Um." She swallowed, looking uncertain for the first time. "I haven't…er…" She pulled a face. "It's just…" She trailed off, looking adorably embarrassed.

Until he figured out what she was trying to say. "Wait." She didn't mean… "What?"

She blew out a breath. "Well, I haven't exactly done this before."

He felt something like frozen. Well, his brain was. Other parts of him were fine and not at all affected by the information, especially when the warmth of her was pressed to the hardness of him, even with the underwear barrier. Will swallowed, but Gracie just kept babbling.

"I was just so focused on becoming a coroner,

and it's a small town so the dating pool is small and then I was hung up on someone there for a while."

Someone. He scowled, surprised at the sharp bolt of jealousy. He didn't consider himself the jealous type. Wouldn't he have figured out Paula was cheating a lot sooner if he had been? "Who were you hung up on?"

She laughed, looking down at him with one of those adorably baffled smiles. "Um, *you*. Have you really not been paying attention?"

"I didn't realize it had been a while." He studied her, the round face, the wavy brown hair, the expressive brown eyes he'd been dreaming about long before he'd admitted to himself she haunted him everywhere. "How long's 'a while'?"

"None of your business," she said primly. Primly while she was straddling him in nothing but her underwear. Then she smiled, as if finding all of her normal poise and strength in the blink of a moment. "But I want it to be you, Will. I want it to be now."

Some little voice in his head told him it was too much, some of that panic he usually felt going to town thrumming through his veins.

But she pressed a kiss to his mouth and it was gone, because she was everything he wanted, and he'd give his life to give her what she wanted. "Gracie. I don't have any sort of protection."

A flush washed up her neck into her cheeks. "I mean, I'm on the pill. So, it'd be... I mean..."

"I haven't been with anyone since Paula."

She smiled at that, some of the flush receding. "Yes, Will, I'm pretty well-aware of that."

"I just meant after the whole cheating thing I got...checked out and, you know, we'd be fine. Everything's fine."

She laughed against his mouth. "We really need to stop talking."

He laughed, too, a real deep laugh and it was such a strange thing to suddenly remember a time when he'd had reason to. A relief and comfort to find it again. To find it with her, and have the promise of a future to keep doing so.

They awkwardly struggled out of their underwear, laughing all the while, and it was in that laughter they came together, each other's names on their lips, a long, slow glide to that connection he hadn't realized he didn't just want, but needed. He needed Gracie in his life—wanted her there, too.

The laughter was gone and there was only her sweetness and warmth. She was pouring hope inside him, filling him with something he'd never truly had before.

She was a sunrise on a new beginning. It didn't erase what had come before, but it made hope spread out like light. When she shuddered against him, he lost himself inside her, determined for this new beginning to be everything they both wanted.

Chapter Fourteen

Gracie couldn't remember ever feeling both so perfectly relaxed and so giddy she just wanted to giggle.

She'd *finally* had sex, and it had been perfect. Amazing. And it had been Will, who dozed next to her, his good arm holding her close.

She should sleep, too. They'd been through so much these past few days, but she was too full of adrenaline and excitement. Too happy.

But happy could end in a moment. She knew that better than most, and she supposed Will did, too.

Nothing had been solved, per se, and she found herself not caring in the slightest bit. Oh, she still wanted to figure it all out, but she wanted this, too. She wanted both: the good and the bad. She wanted a hope for the future, even when things weren't great in the present.

She pressed her cheek to Will's shoulder. She could see the pattern of bruises across his torso, the sharp pop of the white cast against the warmer tones of his skin. His dark blond hair was a tangle, and he needed to shave. He was so handsome, even disheveled and beat up, and somehow this had happened.

A future had happened.

Which meant they had to absolutely figure out the very problematic present, because come Christmas she wanted to celebrate it with the man she loved.

Love. She wanted to laugh out loud again. She wanted to laugh and laugh. She'd fallen in love with Will a while ago, during those glimpses into the man he was. She hadn't let herself really dwell in that, think about that, but it had been there.

Watching him choose to be that man she knew he could be sealed the deal.

She couldn't sleep. Not with love and mysteries battling it out for prominence in her head. As carefully as she could, Gracie slipped out of bed. She needed to move to think, and she needed… A list. She needed to write out the next steps. Just like with work.

Work. Jeez. She pulled on her underwear and her shirt, and then went in search of her pants. Once found, she dug the cell phone out of her pocket. No phone calls or messages. Usually she spent a few days in the office a week, even when things were slow, but she was up to date on all her cases, so unless she got called in there was nothing going on at the moment, and with the holidays a lot of people took time off. Her absence wouldn't be missed as long as she didn't get any calls.

She opened the notes section on her phone and began to pace trying to come up with a to-do list. They needed to contact Kayleigh. Maybe they should look into Jesse. Then there was her uncle who had the same kind of truck and...

She closed her eyes and took a deep breath. There was a lot to look into, but they could only do one thing at a time. She had to prioritize and organize.

"Back to work, huh?" Will murmured sleepily from bed.

She winced and turned to face him sheepishly. "Sorry I woke you."

He shook his head, motioning her back to the bed. "We have to figure this out." He struggled into a sitting position, the blanket falling to his waist, and for a second she just stared at him.

This gorgeous mess of a man was something like hers, and she would do just about anything to protect him. And herself, so that they really got to experience this.

"I made a list," she said, moving to her side of the bed. She scooted next to him and handed it over.

He rubbed a hand over his face before he took the phone and squinted at it. "Okay."

"I start thinking about what to focus on and I get

overwhelmed. I don't know where to start. There are so many threads."

"Well, I'd say we pick one. One at a time. We just have to be methodical. And if you and I are methodical, and Cam is protecting yo— Us," he quickly corrected since she'd been opening her mouth to do so. "And Laurel is pulling her own threads, so we pick one."

"Okay. But which one?"

"I think we follow the Kayleigh Gentry connection. It's a weird long shot but I haven't attempted any weird long shots in two years. Maybe it's time."

"Okay, but I don't think we should call Kayleigh. If she knows something, she might cover it up if we call first. But if we can catch her off guard—"

"And without a cop—"

"Yes. But we can't go back on our word. I know you didn't promise Laurel exactly, but I don't want to wiggle out of that on a technicality. We said we'd work together. We should."

"We can't take a cop with us."

"We need Cam. If Cam came with us as our security, then we'd be staying safe, and we could report it all to Laurel after. She might be irritated, but it isn't going off on our own."

"Okay, but we need Ty, too. To put this Kayleigh woman at ease or have her meet us somewhere."

"One will be easy to use without Laurel's approval. The other?"

A knock sounded on the door and they both froze.

"Gracie? Will? I need to talk to you guys." Laurel's voice was all no-nonsense policewoman.

"Oh my God," Gracie hissed. "I'm pantsless!"

"I'm a lot more than pantsless," Will replied, sounding far too amused.

Gracie scrambled out of bed. "Well, fix it!" she whispered as forcefully as she could.

"I have one arm," Will replied, holding up his cast.

"J-just a second," Gracie called toward the door, her voice too high-pitched. "She's going to know," she muttered, scurrying for her pants.

"Is that a problem?"

Gracie stopped with one leg in her jeans and one leg out. When she'd been thinking about futures she'd been thinking about her and Will and relationship stuff and *love*, not dealing with her overprotective cousins.

He got out of bed, all too perfectly naked, which was quite the momentary distraction. He grabbed his boxers and pulled them on, though she could tell it hurt his arm a little bit.

"You should have a sling."

He raised an eyebrow. "Should I?"

She was an idiot. "And Laurel knowing isn't a

problem exactly. Or it won't be. The timing… Laurel is going to lecture me about the timing."

"So?" he asked with a shrug as he picked up his pants.

"What do you mean 'so'?"

"I mean so what if she lectures you? She's not your boss. You're an adult. She's not in charge of you in any way."

"They look out for me. They took care of me when no one else did. They mean a lot to me. Laurel can be overbearing, but she means well, and she's always been there. It doesn't mean I have to do what she says, but I care. I do have to listen."

"You aren't beholden to the people who love you, Gracie. Not like that."

Laurel knocked again. "What the hell is going on in there? Are you hiding something or… Oh God, Gracie Delaney, you're not… Do I need to come back?"

Gracie had to answer even though Will's seemingly offhanded comment had struck her like a blow. She finished fastening her pants and then she helped Will get his shirt on.

They stood there for a second, Will studying her with one of those unreadable glances she thought sex would magically stop. But there were parts of Will she still didn't understand, and parts of everything she didn't understand. She felt young and stupid and out of her depth.

But Will kissed her temple, light and sweet. "She should respect what you want, because you're smart and determined and have always made good choices. You don't have to prove yourself to her, and if she loves you, she won't want you to, either."

Which was more than a blow. Something like an explosion, and Gracie didn't know how to sort through all the debris so she moved to the door and opened it to Laurel.

Laurel's narrowed gaze went from Gracie to Will. "Can I talk to you in private?" Laurel asked, and even though she was still glaring in Will's direction, everyone knew she was speaking to Gracie.

"I don't really think that's necessary."

Laurel sighed heavily. "I came by to tell you that I'm going to stay here tonight and go over some things with Cam and I thought you might want to join us."

"Of course," Gracie replied overbrightly.

Laurel raised an eyebrow at Will.

"Sure," he said, getting to his feet. "We were just discussing some ideas ourselves."

Laurel rolled her eyes before sailing off into the hallway. Gracie knew she should follow, but she only stood there for a few moments before she felt Will's hand on the small of her back.

"You ready?"

She glanced up at him and there was something about his expression—he was calm and in control, sure, but there was something more. Like he was sincerely asking if she was ready, as if he was really paying attention. It dawned on her that him saying he'd paid attention in spite of himself, or while pretending not to, was true. All this time while she'd thought he'd been clueless he'd just been trying to keep himself separate.

But he hadn't been able to.

She rose to her toes and pressed her mouth to his. "Let's solve this, huh?"

"Sounds like a plan."

WILL SAT ON a couch next to Gracie. Laurel was pacing the floor and Cam was sitting unnaturally still in an armchair.

"You need a presence. This is a police investigation," Laurel said through gritted teeth.

"But you're off duty right now," Will pointed out.

Laurel scowled at him, and he knew he wasn't doing himself any favors in terms of winning over Gracie's family, but someone had to speak the obvious truth. Not to mention the fact they had to play this carefully.

"Whoever messed with my car heard me say something to Gracie in Rightful Claim. Or saw me or something. For two years I've been poking into this. Something had to be the catalyst two years later. We can't be too careful. If Kayleigh has some knowledge we have to be careful it isn't the kind of knowledge that could get her hurt."

Laurel frowned at that, but Will could tell he'd scored a point.

"I think I should go alone. They know what I know. They know I'm a threat. I've already been targeted. Why not keep it focused on one person?"

"Because that puts you in danger again," Gracie said, clearly irritated with his suggestion. "And if they did overhear us at the bar, they've connected me to this, too. If they saw me at your cabin when they set the fire, I'm a target, too."

"Neither of you is going alone or together," Laurel said firmly.

"I have an idea," Gracie said. "One where we all get our way."

Will almost scoffed, but then he looked at Gracie and knew if someone could find a compromise amid all this, it would be her.

"We have Ty meet Kayleigh at Rightful Claim. Laurel and Cam can be there. If you're talking to Grady or pretending to do wedding stuff or something, no one will question it. Will and I can come in and I can go up to Ty to say something, and we can start a very casual conversation. Will can play the obsessed, cuckolded husband and not let anything go. She might give us information, she might not, but it's worth a shot."

"Is that acting?" Laurel asked, her gaze slowly turning to Will.

Maybe because Gracie had just talked about these people protecting her and taking care of her, he could finally understand that Laurel wasn't just a hard-ass cop with no give in her. She cared about Gracie and didn't want her hurt. Which reminded him that he had to care about that, too. If he didn't get along with her cousin, that would hurt Gracie.

So he held Laurel's glare and offered a truth he wasn't 100 percent comfortable voicing, even if it was the truth. "People change, Laurel. Sometimes they get out of the crap that held them down because someone helped them out."

It softened her, clearly and completely.

"It's a good plan," Will said to Gracie. "A good compromise."

"It is," Laurel agreed. "But which one of us is going to get Ty to go along with it?"

All Delaney eyes turned toward Will.

Which was how he found himself outside Rightful Claim at midnight, Gracie at his side. Laurel and Cam had already gone inside when Ty roared up on his motorcycle.

"Hey," he offered as he strode up to the two of

them. "Kayleigh's already inside. Maybe give us a few minutes to get a drink. Relax into it."

"Sure," Gracie said with a nod.

"And just a heads-up, Delaney, Kayleigh's Dad, Jesse Carson, is out of jail. I know you know he takes this feud even more seriously than your uncle, so I'd be careful in there. Maybe just let Will come over and make sure Laurel and Cam stay on their side of the tracks so to speak. You don't want to add any more volatility to this mix."

Will slid a glance to Gracie to find her already looking his way. They both waited to speak until Ty was inside while Christmas lights glittered above and Christmas music quietly soared from inside.

"Why does this one name keep coming up?" Will murmured quietly, watching the streets for anyone who might be paying too much attention or listening too carefully.

"I don't know. There was the man having an affair with Paula, but also the man watching them. Maybe Jesse knows something. Maybe he's the watcher."

"He's been in jail for two years," Will said thoughtfully. "It might explain the timing. It's not that someone overheard us that escalated this. It's that he got out of jail."

"When we go in, you go to Ty and Kayleigh. I'll go to Laurel and see if she can find out what kind of car Jesse drives."

Will nodded. He didn't mention that her uncle could still also be a person of interest, but he supposed he didn't have to. They were all looking for the truth. If Jesse knew something her uncle had done, that would be a truth that came out. That was the important thing.

"Let's go."

She squeezed his hand. "Be careful."

"You, too. No leaving without each other, got it?"

She nodded and tried to pull her hand away, but he wasn't quite ready to let it go. So he pulled her to him instead. She gently placed her hand above his cast. "You need a sling. And probably a checkup."

"When this is all done, we'll figure out both."

She smiled up at him, sweet and hopeful, and he had to believe for the first time in a very long time things would work out okay. One way or another, he would find a way to get this future they were laying the groundwork for.

"I like the sound of *we*," she murmured.

"Me, too." Then he kissed her in the middle of Bent proper, with twinkling lights and quiet music and the odd hush of evening snowfall drifting around them.

Chapter Fifteen

Gracie's heart was beating in overdrive as she and Will dropped each other's hands before stepping into Rightful Claim. There was so much riding on this interaction and she was trying really hard not to get her hopes up, but how could she not?

All they needed was one clear-cut clue and this could be figured out in a matter of hours. But she also knew, through two years of living this mystery, it could stretch on forever.

Laurel and Cam sat at bar stools toward the back, Grady behind the bar. As Gracie walked toward them, Laurel leaned over from her side, Grady leaned in from his and they both grinned at each other.

Gracie wanted that. Laurel and Grady were as different as night and day, as Carsons and Delaneys, but they loved each other. They clicked. Despite the differences. It was special.

Cam watched Gracie as she approached, and she

had no doubt that even though it felt like his eyes were on her, his attention was really focused on the table in the corner where Ty and who she presumed was Kayleigh were sitting.

Will hadn't gone over there yet. He'd gone to the far side of the bar from where Laurel was and ordered a drink from Vanessa Carson, who eyed all the Delaneys on the other end suspiciously while she filled a mug with beer.

"Hey there, AOD," Grady greeted, that razor-sharp Carson grin angled her way.

"Oh, we're shortening it these days." She took a seat next to Laurel. "Cute."

"Well, I like to have nicknames for all the Delaney girls. Laurel here, for instance, is—"

Laurel leaned over the bar and slapped a hand to her fiancé's mouth. "You rethink that line of conversation, Carson, or you will be very, very sorry."

Grady laughed against Laurel's hand and when she finally took it away, he winked in Gracie's direction. "She's crazy about me."

Cam cleared his throat, and both Gracie and Laurel glanced toward the corner. Will was approaching the table where Kayleigh and Ty sat. Ty looked relaxed and polite if uninterested. The blonde who was certainly Kayleigh looked… Well, Gracie didn't know if she was reading into things or what but she suddenly seemed uncomfortable as Will approached.

"I knew Ty wasn't in here for a good time," Grady said, disgustedly glaring at his cousin. "You owe me an explanation later, princess," he muttered before heading down to the other side of the bar and Vanessa.

Gracie looked at Laurel wide-eyed when she didn't pitch a fit at someone calling her princess. "*You* let him call you princess?" she demanded.

Laurel's cheeks flushed pink, but she lifted her chin loftily. "We should focus on the task at hand."

"Uh-huh."

When Laurel and Gracie both looked again at the table in the corner, Cam shook his head. "You two focus on the bar and pretend to be gossiping," Cam said. "They're going to notice if we're all three staring at them."

Gracie turned back around and looked at the drink Grady had placed in front of her. She wasn't going to drink it, so she stole a glance at Laurel, who was doing the same in her direction. "Princess? Really?"

Laurel glared at Gracie this time. "I love the man. Annoying nickname or no. You make certain allowances when you're in love."

Gracie tried not to flush under Laurel's watchful eye.

"You know, love can be confusing. Sometimes incidents can cause people to confuse a certain shared experience or sympathy for—"

"Did I imagine you and Grady falling in love in the midst of you solving a dangerous crime that actually involved you being kidnapped for a bit?"

"That was different."

"How?"

"We didn't have a bunch of dead-wife baggage."

"But you had plenty of Delaney and Carson baggage." Which reminded Gracie of Ty's little tidbit from outside, and the reason they were here, and a much more comfortable subject. "Did you know Jesse Carson is out of jail?"

"Yes, I'd heard. A week ago. I try to keep tabs on that psychopath. I do not trust him."

"His name has come up a few times over the past few days and Will and I were wondering if he's connected to all this somehow. He was Paula's uncle, so not in any affair, but... I don't know. There's all these little clues and none add up, but we should see what kind of car he was driving two years ago. Just to be thorough."

Laurel nodded. "I'll have to go through the proper channels officially for the record, but I might be able to bend a few rules to get that information a little sooner on the down-low." She frowned down at the drink she hadn't touched. "I don't understand any of this."

"I don't, either." Gracie didn't want to add to Laurel's frustration, but it seemed necessary. The more they all knew, the more eyes were on the lookout. This needed to come to an end. "You know who drives that kind of truck."

Laurel's expression shuttered into something blank, and because Gracie at times had to use that expression in her line of work, she knew what it was. It was the mask you put yourself behind when something personal hit. But Gracie wasn't a victim Laurel was trying to solve a case for.

Gracie reached out and put a hand on Laurel's arm. "I don't think it's possible, but I think we have to look at every impossible angle. Especially with the history between him and Jesse."

"We will look at every angle."

"Laurel—"

Laurel quieted her with a steely-eyed glaze. "He's my father, and I love him. But if he did something wrong, that won't change what I have sworn to do or the laws I've promised to uphold. Quite frankly, he was one of the people who instilled that responsibility in me, so if he has *anything* to do with this, I absolutely will make sure he's brought in."

For some reason it made Gracie think about what Will had said earlier. *You aren't beholden to the people who love you.* She had no doubt Laurel would do what was right, but she wondered if she was taking too much of that on herself. "I know you love your job, and you take it very seriously, but there are times when it's okay to step back and let someone else handle something. You don't have to take on every hard thing, especially if it involves people you love."

Laurel stared hard at her hands, which she'd linked together on top of the bar. "If this all connects back to Paula's death, I failed the first time around."

"Hey. You know that isn't true. You know you can't blame yourself when you didn't have the tools or evidence or means necessary to find an answer. We're human."

"Knowing something and feeling something are two different things. You can't tell me that part of why you stuck in Will's life so long was that Paula's death weighed on you even if it wasn't supposed to."

Gracie considered that, but it didn't sit right. Especially with Will's words from earlier about not being beholden to people. Usually she'd accept Laurel's view as truth even if it didn't feel right, but she shouldn't. She shouldn't. "No. It was him. Not her, not the accident. Something about him."

"Uh-oh," Cam muttered, interrupting that moment with Laurel. He swiveled in his seat, ducking his head toward them. "Jesse Carson just walked in."

Laurel swore, hunching herself around her untouched drink. "If he's connected, I don't want him seeing us here. Especially together. One at a time, we split up. Gracie, you go to the bathroom. Text Will to meet you back there once he can extricate himself.

I'll go up to Grady's apartment. Cam, you follow me and go out the back. Watch the front for when Jesse leaves the bar, what he's driving and what direction he's going. Got it?"

Cam and Gracie nodded wordlessly.

"You first, Gracie. Keep your back to the front of the bar, but otherwise keep a leisurely pace. No attention drawing. No panic."

"Yup." She got off her seat and it was hard not to look back, to try to catch a glimpse of Jesse, or to see how Will was faring. But Laurel was right—even without a connection, Jesse was dangerous. They had to take every possible precaution.

She walked into the bathroom, stepped into a stall, then pulled out her phone and texted Will, hoping he wasn't so focused on everything that he ignored his phone.

"WHO'S THIS?" A LARGE, balding man who looked like a stereotypical biker approached. His question was aimed at Kayleigh, and he jammed a thumb in Will's direction as he asked it.

Kayleigh slid her hand over Will's forearm and Will tried not to grimace. He was very much not used to women flirting with him anymore, and the fact she was Paula's cousin and he was almost positive married, based on the ring on her finger, made it extra weird and a little gross.

"This is Will," Kayleigh replied. "What are you doing here, Dad?"

"Got some business to take care of." The man who, if he was Kayleigh's dad, had to be Jesse Carson, eyed Will. "I know you?"

"Maybe," Will returned with a casual shrug as he carefully pulled his arm away from Kayleigh. He hadn't gotten much out of the woman. She kept going on about how talking about Paula made her too sad, or how the past was best left in the past. Even with Ty's casual attempts at moving the conversation toward Paula, she didn't bite.

Something about it was off, that Will knew, and the appearance of Kayleigh's father confirmed all his suspicions. If only he could figure out what any of his suspicions actually meant.

Maybe Jesse was the answer.

"I was married to Paula," Will offered when Jesse still said nothing else. "We didn't attend a lot of Carson family functions, so I'm not sure we would have ever run into each other. But you were her uncle, right?"

Jesse grunted, narrowing his eyes at Kayleigh, and then at Ty. "So, who's gonna go get me a celebratory get-out-of-jail drink? Ty? I'll take something hard. Have Grady put it on my tab."

Ty rolled his eyes, but he got up to do Jesse's bidding nonetheless.

"And you," he said, giving Kayleigh an intimidating glare. "You have to go to the bathroom."

"Excuse me?" she all but screeched.

"Do as you're told, girl. Or I'll tell Cyrus a few things I don't think you want your husband to hear about."

Kayleigh huffed, muttering things about being an adult and not being bullied by her jerk of a dad, but she got up off her stool. "Whatever," she muttered.

Will nearly jumped when her hand drifted across his butt as she walked behind him to go to the bathroom.

Jeez. He pretended to watch her go, but he was really scanning the bar for Delaneys, who had scattered and disappeared. He frowned and turned back to Jesse.

"Looking for something?" Jesse demanded gruffly. "Maybe a few someones."

"Huh?" Something was off and weird. Why was this man maneuvering people so they were alone?

"I hear you've been looking into Paula's death, that you think it's shady. That true?"

Will's throat felt dry but he took a sip of his beer and did his best to keep the building panic under wraps. "Never settled right with me. The way she died."

"Me neither. I've been in jail, of course, but I had methods of investigation from the inside."

Will didn't trust this man, but all of this could lead him somewhere. "What exactly are you saying?"

Jesse leaned close. "I have information. Evidence. And it all ties back to your girlfriend's uncle."

Will's body went to ice. Not just because Jesse was implicating Gracie's uncle, but that he knew or assumed a relationship had developed there. He didn't like Gracie being on this man's radar, especially when tied to this. It hadn't occurred to him it might be used to hurt her, and for the first time he regretted grabbing life by the horns before solving this mystery.

"You want the information," Jesse continued in that low, conspiring tone. "Then you and the girl-friend meet me outside in ten."

"I don't know what you're—"

"And if you don't, I guess you're just out of luck." With that, Jesse gave him a hard pat on his broken arm that had Will hissing in pain.

Jesse laughed as he sauntered out of Rightful Claim.

As much as Will didn't trust Jesse, he couldn't think of any reason Jesse would have to lie. To say he had evidence when he didn't. He searched the room again, but all the Delaneys were missing. What the hell?

He fished his phone out of his pocket to find a message from Gracie.

Meet me in the back by the bathrooms.

He immediately moved for the back, trying to ignore the searing pain in his arm. Kayleigh bounded out of the bathroom and though Will tried to do a sidestep that would keep her from seeing him, she pounced.

"Hey, sweetheart. Dad gone?" She grabbed on to his good arm.

Will tried to extricate himself, but she only scooted closer, cornering him against the wall as she trailed a fingertip up the zipper of his coat.

"Look, I have to—"

The women's bathroom door swung open again and Gracie stepped out. *Thank God.* "I have to talk to my girlfriend." He slid away from Kayleigh's body.

She scowled after him, and then at Gracie. "A Delaney? You can't be serious."

"It was nice seeing you, Kayleigh. See you around and all that." Will waved awkwardly and walked over to where Gracie was standing by the door frowning. "Save me," he whispered.

That frown didn't leave her face, and she studied him, then slowly turned her gaze to Kayleigh.

"Aren't you married to Cyrus Gentry?" Gracie asked, as if she was totally confused by the whole situation.

Will didn't think she was.

Kayleigh huffed and turned on a heel, stalking back out to the main portion of the bar. Before Will could tell Gracie what Jesse had said, she peered up at him.

"*Am* I your girlfriend?"

Will rocked back on his heels, taken completely off guard by the question. "Er. Well, I mean, we slept together. Which was a first for you. I should hope I'm something to you."

Her mouth curved, a small self-satisfied smile. He wished he had the time or place to enjoy it. "We have to go."

"What?"

"Jesse told me he has evidence, but he'll only give it to me if we meet him outside." He took her arm and started propelling her toward the front. "Where did the other two go?"

"We didn't want Jesse to see us." She pulled her arm away, stopping them before they got into the thick of the bar. "We need to get Laurel before we go out there."

"There's no time. I don't know how long he's going to wait, and he said it was this or nothing. Text her as we walk out there."

"Cam's waiting outside to watch Jesse," Gracie said, pulling her phone out of her pocket. "So we won't be out there alone. Let's go out the back."

Will nodded and followed her to the back exit.

Chapter Sixteen

They stepped out into the back. It was weirdly dark, no Christmas or parking lights shining. It didn't make sense, but Gracie was never out this late. Maybe there was some reasonable explanation.

The door to the bar snapped shut and they were plunged into almost complete darkness. Will stopped walking, holding Gracie to get her to stop, as well. "Something isn't—"

Someone in the dark snatched her phone out of her hand before she could hit Send on the text to Laurel. She reached out for whoever it was but found nothing but air. "Hey!"

"You won't be needing that," a low voice said, far too close to her ear. She moved closer to Will, but she could tell she accidentally jarred his broken arm by the way he hissed in a breath and she jumped back.

"Jesse, if you have evidence—"

"I'm in charge here, son. You'd do good to remember that."

It was all wrong. Even though it was dark when it shouldn't have been, Cam should be here. He was supposed to watch Jesse. Even if Cam was staying out of sight, he would have noticed the light situation and done something. Warned her or gotten Laurel or done something.

Now Jesse had her phone, and she might have written it off as threatening bullying but too much was wrong and off.

"I want my phone back," Gracie said, determined to be strong and pretend like nothing was wrong.

"Little Delaney bitch wants her phone back. We all want something, sweetheart. Delaneys are finally going to be out of luck."

"That's enough," Will said, a dangerous growl to his voice.

But Gracie knew they weren't in control here. This was all wrong and they were in the weaker position. She tried to reach back for the door behind her, but a meaty hand curled around her arm.

"Let go of me," she warned.

"Sorry, sweetheart. You're coming with me."

She tried to wrench her arm free, and she could feel Will moving forward. But there was a sickening crack of something, and then a thud.

"Will?" she whispered, suddenly boneless with fear, thoughts of fighting back disappearing as she tried to reach out for Will.

But Jesse's grip only tightened.

"Might live through that. Might not." Jesse's voice was low and pleased. Gracie's stomach turned as he started dragging her away.

She fought. Kicked and jerked and pulled, but he was so much stronger than her. When he got to a truck, the engine roared to life and as he jerked open the passenger-side door, the dome light came on to reveal Kayleigh Gentry in the driver's seat.

What the hell was happening?

But Jesse hefted Gracie easily and tossed her into the truck. She tried to scramble back out immediately, but he blocked her with his body as he slid into the passenger seat.

With the light, she could fight back more effectively, but Kayleigh slammed on the accelerator and the unexpected movement of the truck caused Gracie to fall forward into the dash. Which allowed Jesse the chance to grab her arms again and pull them behind her back. He pulled her onto his lap and Gracie struggled to free herself, but he only laughed.

Then his voice was in her ear. "You don't want to excite me, sweetheart."

She nearly retched right there. But she stilled. She could kick across at the steering wheel or Kayleigh's leg on the accelerator to make Kayleigh crash, but there was too much risk she'd die since she was sitting this close to the windshield. She could keep fighting Jesse, but he could outmuscle her so easily it was a waste of energy.

She'd have to wait it out. She knew Bent and the surrounding areas as well as anyone. They couldn't take her anywhere she wouldn't know how to escape from. As long as she could escape Jesse's too-tight grip, she might have a chance.

Then there was the fact Jesse had her phone. If it was still on, it was possible Laurel could trace it even if Gracie couldn't get a message to her.

She had to calm herself. She had to focus. Except she kept going back to that sickening crack and the thud afterward. What about Will? Would someone find him there in the dark?

"What did you do to Will?"

"Nothing your family hasn't done to mine," Jesse replied as if they were discussing the weather.

She wanted to ask about Cam, but she was afraid that might tip them off. She had to hope Cam was unharmed and had seen them take her and was following. Or something. The less these two knew about which Delaneys knew what, the better.

"I don't know what I have to do with this," Gracie said, trying to do her best to sound calm and unafraid. "Or how you're involved in Paula's death, or—"

Jesse laughed, squeezing her wrists so tight she whimpered.

"I did what I had to do to protect my family. To

stand up for them. And somehow *I* ended up in jail when your uncle is the one who deserves so much worse than that." Jesse's evil smile glinted in the headlights of an oncoming car. "Now I finally have the means to make him pay and pay."

She wanted to cry, or scream, but neither would help her any. Or Will. God, Will. The only way she could help him was to survive and get out of here. So instead she paid attention to where they were going. Down Main, like it was the most normal thing in the world.

But it could be good. Maybe people would see them. Laurel would have to come searching for them soon, and she would have people who had witnessed where they went.

Of course it was late and Bent was pretty much closed down for the night and—

Positive thoughts. There was no room for negativity. She had to get through this, so she had to believe she could.

Kayleigh drove out of town, but not far. It only took a few more minutes for Gracie to realize she wasn't being taken to some off-the-beaten-path, hidden-away place at all. They were driving right up to the Delaney Ranch.

"What is this?" she demanded as Kayleigh drove onto Delaney property, as if this had been their planned destination all along.

"Would have preferred your cop cousin, honestly," Jesse said, something like black, evil excitement twisting his features. "I knew it'd be a lot easier to get you though, and I don't have the time to be picky anymore. Your uncle will think twice before messing with my family again."

Gracie swallowed. "If you think I mean anything to him, I hate to break it to you—"

"Damn Delaneys are always so naive. He doesn't need to love you, little girl. You're a Delaney. Blood is all that matters. It's all that ever will."

THERE WAS A BLACKNESS. A terrible pain. Was he back on the side of that road? His arm sure hurt badly enough, but there was something hard on it. And the person calling his name, over and over, the fingertips touching him, it wasn't Gracie.

If it wasn't Gracie, the blackness seemed like a better place to stay.

But something wasn't right about that. Because Gracie wasn't here. She should be here. Where was she?

He struggled to open his eyes, to move. Someone was saying his name. It just wasn't Gracie.

"He's coming to," the woman said. "You both need an ambulance."

"No one is getting in an ambulance until we figure out where Gracie is. He'll need stitches, but there's no major damage," a man's voice said.

They didn't know where Gracie was, and that made him fight the darkness even harder.

"You're not a doctor, Cam," the woman said—Laurel. It had to be Laurel talking. And she was talking to Cam, who was the man's voice.

"I dealt with plenty of medical emergencies as a marine. He'll live. How long will the trace take?"

"They have to contact the phone company. Once they get through, it should be soon."

Will tried to speak, but his tongue felt five times its normal size and he couldn't make any part of his body move. God, his arm hurt almost as badly as when it had been originally broken. He had a sudden flash of Jesse hitting it inside the bar.

Jesse. He tried to speak again. "Jesse. Jesse took her."

Laurel peered down at him. They were outside in the parking lot, but there were lights now. Laurel had a flashlight, too. "We're pinging her phone. Presuming she has it. Will, are you okay?"

"Jesse has it. The phone. He has it."

"Good. Even better to ping him. Did he say anything? Anything at all that could give us some idea of what's happening or where they were going?"

It was fuzzy. Flashes here and there. He glanced at Cam and frowned. The man had a dried streak of blood from his temple down his cheek. "You're bleeding."

"Lead pipe to the temple. Just like you. Yours is worse."

"I want to sit up."

"You need a hospital," Laurel said. "This is probably your second concussion in a few days. You both need a hospital."

"I'll live," he said, struggling to get up. Cam ended up helping him. He was woozy, nauseous, but Gracie was missing. *Missing.* With that giant man who'd hit both him and Cam with a lead pipe.

"Why didn't he just kill us?" Will muttered, feeling like he'd been bruised and battered. Well, he supposed he had been.

"Murder is a little more jail time than battery," Cam replied. "But he's certainly racking the charges up. Can you remember anything?"

"He came in. He made Ty and Kayleigh leave, and you were all gone."

"We didn't want him to see us," Laurel replied. "The three of us in a Carson bar, even with me engaged to Grady, is just a little too weird."

"I think he knew." Will took a deep breath and let it out. It seemed to help with the nausea and the pain, but not with the roiling fear that Gracie was with that lunatic. "Or something."

"Yeah, he knew something enough to take me out using Kayleigh as a damn diversion," Cam muttered, clearly disgusted with himself.

"He was talking about Delaneys, something about Delaneys getting what they deserve, but I can't figure out what he meant exactly, or why he'd want to take Gracie. We have to find her."

"The department is going to call me as soon as they have the trace information."

Laurel sounded so calm, seemed so absolutely fine with her cousin being kidnapped by a psychopath, and he might have yelled at her for that but he saw the way her hand trembled before she curled it into a fist and stood.

"We need to get inside. You're both freezing and hurt."

But just as she said it, the door opened and Grady stepped out. "Carson grapevine worked. Someone saw Jesse's truck on the road up to the Delaney Ranch."

"Why would he go there?"

"Wish I knew. You sure they don't need an ambulance?" Grady asked, nodding toward him and Cam.

He probably did. He felt worse than he had after the car accident, and he hadn't thought that was possible.

But Gracie was out there. And Jesse was taking her to Delaney property.

"We all have to go," Will said, trying to get to his

feet. It took the wall and Cam's help to get him there, but after a few woozy seconds things smoothed out. "We have to go."

"I don't want to take my cruiser, or your truck for that matter, Cam. Both are way too conspicuous."

"What about Gracie's truck? Isn't it at Carson Auto? Doubt Jesse would know it. Unless he's the one who shot the window out. Even then, it's fairly nondescript."

"I'll go ask Van," Grady said, immediately disappearing back inside.

"I guess he didn't smash your brain completely to bits," Laurel offered, sounding a little surprised.

"Laurel, Cam, I know you aren't going to want to hear this, but this somehow connects to your father. I don't know how. I really don't. But after all these little threads, and now Jesse Carson is headed for your father. He connects."

"If he connects, then we will deal with that. I promise you."

Vanessa Carson came out the door, and made a quick hand motion. "Follow me to the shop. Faster to walk probably. Gracie's truck is fixed."

"Thanks, Vanessa," Laurel said, but Vanessa just grunted.

Laurel and Vanessa moved at rapid speed down the boardwalk to Carson Auto. Will's head and arm ached and burned with every step, but he thought of

Gracie. Alone. In the middle of something that had nothing to do with her.

By the time Will and Cam caught up with Laurel, she was already sliding into the driver's seat. Cam went for the front seat, so Will used his good arm to awkwardly open the back door. Damn, everything hurt.

Vanessa pulled a face at the awkward, overly gentle way he and Cam moved. "You two look like crap."

"Yeah, thanks," Will muttered, sliding into the back seat. Laurel was pulling out of the garage before Will even had the door closed and all he could do was lean back in the seat and hope like hell they could solve this once and for all.

All that really mattered was that Gracie was safe and unhurt. He couldn't even consider the possibility of anything else because it hurt worse than his many injuries.

Laurel's phone went off. She pulled the phone to her ear. "Delaney."

Will strained to hear whatever the person on the other end was saying, but it was no use. The few seconds that passed were agony, even as Laurel drove them toward the Delaney Ranch.

She dropped the phone. "Pinged at the ranch house." She swore, a rare sign of emotion. "What the hell is Jesse Carson doing?"

"Feuding," Cam returned darkly.

"That's not an answer."

"It's not a reasonable answer. But it's an answer."

"It connects to Paula," Will said firmly.

"Paula is a Carson," Cam pointed out. "Maybe Jesse believes what you do. That someone killed her. This is revenge. He thinks it was a Delaney."

Will didn't want to say it, but it was important. "Look, it could have been a Delaney. The woman at the motel said the man having an affair with my wife drove a black—"

"Gracie told me," Laurel said quietly. If there was emotion in her over her father being implicated, she didn't show it. "At the bar. She told me Dad might be involved."

"He could have been having an affair with Paula. It's possible."

"He's just as big of a hater of the Carsons as Jesse is of him. I can't imagine him messing around with one. Let alone a married one."

"Okay, well, maybe he wasn't. Maybe Jesse only thinks he was. The truth isn't as important as whatever Jesse thinks is the truth. It has to connect, or he wouldn't have used me as part of it." A memory slapped him, hard and painful, and Will couldn't believe it had slipped away. "Wait. He told me. He told me when he talked to me he had evidence your father was involved. That's how he lured us outside."

Laurel pulled through the archway to the Delaney

Ranch, a determined set to her jaw. "Well, we're about to find out the truth, one way or another."

"Nothing is more important than Gracie not being hurt. Not even the truth," Will insisted.

Laurel turned off the lights and pulled Gracie's car off the drive up to the house. Though the night was dark, the Christmas lights of the main house and a cabin off in the distance lit their drive. Instead of heading for the main house, Laurel drove toward a cabin on the far side of the property.

She stopped the car behind the cabin, hiding them from the view from the main house. She turned to Will.

"Gracie is the most important thing, which is why we need to have a plan before we head in there. A plan we all agree to follow no matter what. A plan that minimizes surprise and damage. Once she's out, we'll find the truth. Period. But no one risks themselves."

Will couldn't make that promise. He'd risk himself a thousand times over to keep Gracie safe.

Chapter Seventeen

Gracie was shaking. She didn't know if it was fear or cold, or possibly both, but she couldn't stop it no matter how many times Jesse warned her to knock it off. They had been crouched in the snow next to the porch of the Delaney house for she didn't know how long. Jesse had tied her hands together, with just enough extra rope so that he could hold on to the end of it and jerk her this way and that or pull her like a dog.

Gracie couldn't take it anymore. "He's asleep. Are we going to wait here all night? You'll freeze to death just as much as I will."

"Shut your mouth, girl." He jerked her rope so hard she fell over without her arms to break the fall. The ground was hard and the snow was cold and piercing.

Jesse and Kayleigh laughed like it was a good-natured prank.

It made her want to give up, but she knew she couldn't do that. She and her uncle might not be close, but she couldn't let Jesse hurt him. And what if no one had found Will? What if Cam was hurt, too? There was too much riding on her surviving. She couldn't let the Carsons' cruelty get to her.

Gracie struggled onto her knees. In the distance she thought she heard a car engine. It could be her imagination, a desperate hallucination. It could also be a truck on the highway in the distance—they usually didn't hear traffic up here but it was a cold night. Engine noise could travel. But she didn't want to take the chance it might be help, and the Carsons might see or hear it and hurt whoever could possibly be coming for her. So she started coughing. Coughing and coughing, even when Jesse told her to shut up and jerked the rope again.

She simply fell into the snow and coughed some more.

Jesse swore up and down, threatening her with all sorts of things, but she didn't stop coughing. She had to try to mask the sound just in case.

When Jesse kicked her in the ribs, hard, she squeaked at the sharp, unexpected blast of pain. She had to stop coughing because it hurt too much and it was taking everything she had to try to breathe through the crushing pain in her ribs.

"Are you sure you sent it to the right number?"

Jesse demanded of Kayleigh, though Gracie had no idea what Kayleigh was supposed to have sent. There was some kind of plan they'd clearly devised before they'd taken her, and Gracie couldn't figure any of it out. Most especially why they were here.

Before Kayleigh could answer her father, a light inside flipped on. It illuminated the satisfied grin on Jesse's face and if Gracie wasn't in so much pain she might have had the wherewithal to get more afraid.

Jesse pulled her by the rope and didn't give her a chance to get to her feet. He dragged her through the snow as she wriggled and struggled to find a way to get up. It was only once they got to the porch that he stopped dragging her through the snow.

She tried not to sob, even though that was what she wanted to do. This was painful and demoralizing and she didn't understand how she was in the thick of it. Jesse jerked her to her feet just as the front door opened.

Her uncle stood there looking as polished as he ever did. His short hair didn't have one sleep-flattened section, and he wore a robe like most men wore a suit. He looked at the trio of them with regal superiority.

When his gaze met hers, some of that faltered for one second before it smoothed back out. "Grace," he said in that disappointed tone she'd known all of her life with him. He frowned at her. "I should have known it would come down to you."

Gracie didn't have a response. She didn't have anything. She could only stumble forward as Jesse pushed her inside.

"Carson, I don't know what you think you're doing, but surely you know it's only going to end in jail time. Again." He looked at Kayleigh with that sneer of disgust Gracie didn't think he was trying to hide at all. "And bringing your daughter into it. You've made a misstep here."

"Have I?" Jesse asked, studying the vast living room bathed in a warm glow from the chandelier above. The Christmas tree lights were off, but the prettily decorated tree stood big and full in the corner, cheerful and mocking.

Jesse jerked the rope again and this time it propelled Gracie forward into an end table, sending a shooting pain up her leg and knocking over a lamp in the process. It crashed to the ground.

Jesse sat on the couch, still grinning, as he jerked the rope again. Gracie was ready for it this time so she didn't fall, but she did have to take the steps toward the couch as he pulled on the rope.

"What is this about, Carson? It's the middle of the night. Some of us are gainfully employed and have meetings in the morning."

Gracie wished she could be shocked he was so calm, so completely unconcerned with the fact Jesse had her tied up like a rabid animal, but all in all it was about as much as she could expect from her uncle.

"This is about revenge, Delaney. It's about your people stealing everything my people were ever owed. It's about the crap hand we've been dealt by Delaneys since the beginning of Bent."

Uncle Geoff sighed heavily. "I'll never understand why the lazy, shiftless Carson clan has convinced themselves they're owed anything when they won't do a hard day's work to save their lives."

Jesse only smiled, and that was when Gracie knew this was very, very bad. Because she expected him to rage. To pounce. To fight. Every Carson she'd ever come into contact with who was obsessed with the feud was always ready to brawl. Usually because a Delaney had done exactly what her uncle had done— been a condescending jerk.

But Jesse was calm. Happy. It was all so very scary and even as she worked to get her hands out of their bonds, she knew they were too tight.

"I have proof you were involved in the crash that killed Paula Cooper."

Uncle Geoff scoffed. "I didn't kill anyone."

Jesse laughed, an edge of bitterness and something else Gracie had a bad feeling was insanity.

"No. Of course not. Wouldn't want to get your hands dirty. But it just so happens I know who killed

Paula, and with that knowledge, I can make sure the police think you did it."

Geoff's face was expressionless, but Gracie knew enough to understand that only meant he had some deep, violent emotion he was hiding.

It occurred to her that by witnessing this, hearing this, Jesse's intent was not to use her as a pawn. He was going to kill her. Because if she knew he was framing Geoff, she couldn't possibly be trusted to live.

The panic beat so hard she could barely hear what they were saying over it, and it seemed the more she struggled against the rope holding her hands together, the tighter and more unbearable it got.

"Don't think for a second your precious daughter can stop that from happening," Jesse was saying. "No one is going to let her weasel you out of this. I'm going to put you in jail just like you put me in jail."

"You put yourself in jail when you robbed one of my tellers. As for Laurel, unlike Carsons, Delaneys have morals and standards. Which means Laurel will seek the truth. I don't need her to get me out of a lie, because your lie will be discovered. Honestly you think you'd learn at some point you can't hurt me, Carson. I'm untouchable, and smarter than you."

Gracie winced, not at the bonds this time, but at the way her uncle was poking at this angry, vicious man while he had her in his mercy.

"Morals and standards," Jesse repeated, rubbing a hand over his chin. Gracie watched the other hand hoping against hope his grip on the rope loosened. "Is that why you were sneaking away to hotel rooms with my married niece?"

Gracie waited for her uncle to deny it. To use that same calm, assured voice to say it wasn't true. Jesse was mistaken or lying again.

But he merely looked grim.

"Oh my God," Gracie whispered, staring at her uncle's face. He didn't look at her, nothing in his gaze changed, but she knew it had to be true. *He'd* slept with Paula. Jesse had been the man watching them.

"No matter," Jesse said happily. "What's incredibly immoral is killing, and you're about to kill your niece. A shame for both of you."

"What on earth? You have lost your mind, Carson. I'm not going to kill Grace. You can't make me."

"A niece for a niece. It's only fair. I had to end Paula's life, you have to end this one."

Gracie tried not to react, but she shook harder nonetheless. Jesse had killed Paula.

The blood had drained out of Geoff's face. "You killed Paula. Why would you…"

"I warned her. I warned her that if she let a Delaney touch her again she'd face the consequences. They were a little more dire than I'd planned, but she brought it upon herself. So, still your fault. Now, let's get on with it. Kayleigh?"

Kayleigh produced two guns from her purse and handed them to Jesse. He laughed, low and oh so pleased with himself.

"See, the beauty of my plan is that I don't have to make you kill your niece. I only have to kill her, and make it look like you did. Two murders? Oh, you're going to rot for a very long time."

"I SHOULD HAVE made you two go to the hospital," Laurel whispered irritably as they finally made it to the house. Both he and Cam had encountered mild dizzy spells on the trek through the snow, causing them both to fall, but they'd gotten back up. They were both upright.

As for Will, he was upright with a pounding headache and a roiling nausea settled in his gut, but he wasn't about to stop. Gracie was in that house somewhere, in danger. He'd deal with his injuries once she was safe.

"We're fine," Cam said shortly, and Will knew if he said it himself it would sound hollow and weak compared to Cam's forceful military surety. So he kept his mouth shut.

"The lights are on. Dad's the only one home and it's two in the morning. What on earth is this if they've got the lights on?"

Cam moved toward the window, but unless marines had X-ray vision he wasn't going to see anything. All the curtains were drawn.

"We have to go in there," Will said. It felt like stating the obvious, but both Cam and Laurel were clearly more predisposed to caution.

"We have to be careful," Laurel countered.

Screw caution. Will knew she was a cop and used to tense, dangerous situations, but he didn't know how she could stay calm or *out here* when Gracie was inside.

"I'm going in there." He didn't have to listen to these people or take orders from anyone, and he wasn't letting Gracie be at the mercy of any of those people.

"You're hurt and one man. If you bash in there you're likely to get both of you killed. And possibly our father."

"Or he's involved."

Neither Laurel nor Cam said anything to that, and he'd give them a little credit for not immediately jumping to their father's defense.

"We need to do this tactically. One person stays outside to assess the situation while two people move in from two different entry points," Cam said.

"Laurel should stay outside," Will said firmly. When she started to protest, Will just kept talking. "You've called backup, and you need to apprise them of the situation. Besides, you're bound by certain regulations. Cam and I aren't."

"He has a point," Cam said, pulling a set of keys out of his pocket. "I'll take the garage side entry, and Will can go in the back. Laurel stays here in the front. We'll assess the situation inside and then report immediately back. No heroics, just information gathering. As long as things aren't dire, we'll come back out and wait for more police."

"Will doesn't have a weapon."

"He doesn't need one if we're just information gathering."

Of course, Will wasn't planning on just information gathering, but they didn't need to know that. Maybe they had the patience to wait around and *assess* situations, but Will couldn't damn well breathe knowing Gracie was in danger.

Cam handed him a key. "This will get you in the back door. You'll be in a mud room, the door will likely be closed. On the other side of that door is the kitchen, which opens up into the living room. It appears the living room lights are the only ones on, so I wouldn't venture past the kitchen. Just try to see who's in the living room and listen if you can hear any conversation. All we're doing is figuring out what's going on. Remember, Gracie can hold her own."

Of course she could. But she shouldn't have to.

So Will didn't say anything—he just started walking around the giant house, fighting against the dizziness and nausea plaguing him. He could give in to that later. Once Gracie was safe.

He made it to the door, cold and somehow exhausted. Everything felt about three times harder since Jesse had knocked him out, but he had to keep pushing. As carefully as he could with shaking hands and double vision, Will managed to get the key into its hole.

Another deep breath and then he pushed inside with as much finesse as he could manage. The room was mostly dark, except a slight sliver of light that snuck in through the door. Cam had said it led to the kitchen.

Will crept toward it and then reached out to slowly pull it open enough so he could slip through the crack. It creaked as he moved it, and in the thundering silence of his own mind it sounded supersonic. He froze.

He froze and he waited and nothing happened. He heard no footsteps, no voices. Just his own ragged breath and his heartbeat drumming in his ears. Once he got that mildly under control, he moved through the small opening he'd managed. The door squeaked again, but he had to believe he wouldn't be heard this time any more than he'd been heard the first.

He crept through the kitchen toward the opening

on the far side. The one that supposedly led to the living room, where the lights were on.

The light from the living room was bright enough if anyone came into the kitchen they would definitely see him. Which had him looking around the perfectly clean, ridiculously expensive-looking kitchen for some kind of weapon. He'd prefer a gun, but a knife would have to do.

He slid a butcher's knife out of the knife block on the counter, then crept toward the opening again. The closer he got to the opening, the more he could hear voices.

Low and very nearly calm. At least they sounded calm, but then Jesse laughed, low and dangerous, and Will knew there was nothing calm about what was going on.

He edged as close as he could without risking being seen.

"See, the beauty of my plan," Jesse was saying, in that same casual voice that Will could only regard as wildly out of place and maybe a little psychotic, "is that I don't have to make you kill your niece. I only have to kill her, and make it look like you did."

It took a moment for those words to make any sense. They still didn't even as Will stepped forward into the opening to the living room. It didn't need to make full sense to know that Gracie was in trouble.

And barging in, knowing Jesse was likely armed,

would only get them all killed. He had to do something without drawing attention. Something to give him some kind of advantage or just even footing. He had to get Gracie out of there.

Holding his breath, he looked out the opening of the kitchen. Will took in the scene. Jesse lounging on a couch as Kayleigh handed him not one but two guns. Gracie's uncle standing next to a chair looking calm and collected if a little pale.

It took Will a few more seconds to find Gracie, sitting on the floor, hands tied behind her back while the end of the rope was held tightly in Jesse's fist.

There was only one light on. A giant chandelier hanging from above. He'd only need to get the light off to find some kind of advantage, or maybe spur Cam and Laurel into action. Jesse would still have a grip on Gracie, but it would be harder for him to hurt her, and Will had a straight shot to her if he didn't get disoriented.

He looked to the left wall, searching for a light switch. Nothing. As he turned his head to look to the other side of the wall, he had the misfortune of catching Kayleigh's gaze.

Her eyes widened. "Daddy," Kayleigh said, a kind of whispery tone as if she didn't believe what she was seeing.

Will looked away, diving toward the right wall and a row of light switches. He slapped his hand against them, flicking them all off, hoping against hope he'd found the right switch.

When they were plunged into darkness, he didn't have time to sigh in relief. A gunshot went off.

Chapter Eighteen

Gracie screamed when the gun went off. But there was no sound after it. No moan of pain or thud of someone falling over.

Oh God. She prayed with everything she had that the bullet missed everyone in the room.

She didn't have time to pray for long. Not tied up in a room with two people who wanted her dead. She jerked her hands and body as hard as she could and nearly sobbed in triumph when she'd clearly caught Jesse off guard enough for him to let the rope go.

She rolled, trying to keep a clear picture of the room in her head. When she stopped, hoping she was at least somewhat near the front door, she realized the entire room was silent. She could occasionally hear a shuffle, an intake or outtake of breath, but no one was talking.

Which only made her heart pound harder. The curtains were drawn, letting none of the lights outside shine in, so she couldn't see anything. Getting to the door was possible, but if she opened the front door it would draw attention to where she was. She doubted Jesse would be afraid to shoot indiscriminately. Really her only hope was that he had some concern for his daughter, and she had to wonder about that since he'd involved her in this whole thing.

Who had turned off the lights though? Had it been an accident? There were too many questions. Too many what-ifs.

But Jesse hadn't had a chance to kill her, so there was that. She reached out, feeling the floor around her and trying to get a better gauge of where she was in the room.

"All right, who turned off the lights?" Jesse's voice growled, and Gracie was somewhat relieved at how far away his voice sounded. She'd gotten some distance from him.

"It was Will Cooper," Kayleigh said, her voice shrill and maybe a little frightened. "That bastard came in through the kitchen."

Gracie nearly gasped with relief. Will was alive. Will was *here*.

"Thought I killed him," Jesse said, and Gracie would never get used to the conversational way he discussed killing and hurting people.

Will. Will was here. Suddenly relief and happiness at him being alive morphed into fear. Now that was two people she cared about in danger, and she had absolutely no clue how to save any of them.

A phone. She had to get to a phone. If it was in its base, there should be one in the far corner by the kitchen entry, and maybe if she headed that way she could find Will. Either way, if she could get a phone and dial 911... Maybe it would lead Jesse to her, the movement or the sound, but she had to try.

She started crawling in what she hoped was the right direction and as she moved she realized she could hear shuffling getting closer and closer.

Something brushed her hand, followed by a sharp intake of breath. "Gracie?" someone whispered. Will. It *had* to be Will. It definitely wasn't her uncle, and Kayleigh and Jesse wouldn't whisper.

When a warm hand touched her shoulder, she was 100 percent certain it was Will. She didn't want to answer since the room had fallen silent again, so she reached out with her other hand and put it on top of his on her shoulder. She felt his whoosh of relieved breath, but it was also too loud in the quiet room.

"Kayleigh, get over to me and then I'm going to start shooting and hope I hit something."

Kayleigh said something in return, but Gracie couldn't hear it because Will was whispering in her ear.

"Can you get us to the front door?"

She carefully turned her mouth to his ear, doing

her best to whisper as softly as possible while Jesse and Kayleigh bickered as they tried to find each other.

"We can't leave my uncle."

"Laurel's outside. Police on their way. Cam's somewhere. We need to get you out and let the others handle the rest."

Gracie swallowed. Help was here. A lot of it. She squeezed his hand and then maneuvered herself, hopefully back toward the door. She put Will's bad hand on her back, hoping he got the hint she was going to guide him to as close to the front door as she could manage.

They moved along, and as she moved she listened to Jesse and Kayleigh practically yelling at each other at this point.

"How can you not find me, girl? We weren't that far apart? Don't make me start shooting without you."

"I can't see anything!" Kayleigh cried in return. "I cannot believe you'd threaten to shoot me. What kind of father are you?"

"What kind of useless are you that you still sound far away?" Jesse demanded, a cruel, awful growl to his voice.

Gracie picked up her pace. She didn't doubt Jesse might snap and start shooting indiscriminately if

Kayleigh didn't reach his side soon. She reached out to crawl forward, but found wall. Not door. Wall.

She didn't let herself panic, though she wanted to cry in frustration. Instead, she started feeling along the wall, trying to find a hint of anything that might give her a clue as to where she was.

Her hands brushed a hard corner. She felt around it, determining it was the windowsill. There were the curtains. But which side of the window was she on?

She tried to count her breathing and focus on that over fear that silence had descended again. *Inhale, one two three. Exhale, one two three.*

She nearly cried out when her fingertips ran from wall to another hard edge. The door frame. Oh, thank God. She felt along until her hand found the doorknob. She reached back and took Will's hand, leading it to the doorknob, as well.

His hand closed over hers and his mouth was at her ear again. "I'm going to open it. You're going to go out and find Laurel."

"What about you?"

"I'll be behind you."

She swallowed, then squeezed his hand again, a nonverbal yes. She pulled away, on her hands and knees to the side of the door so Will could pull it open.

She heard something click, and the door squeaked as it opened, a little shaft of Christmas light glow edging through. It would draw attention, but Gracie didn't hesitate. She crawled out the opening onto the cold cement of the porch. She turned to help Will out, but the door closed instead.

Then it exploded as a bullet smashed through it.

And into her.

WILL COULD ONLY SIT, frozen and in shock that the bullet hadn't hit him. He'd felt it whizz by him, and then heard the exploding crash of it smashing through the door.

The door Gracie had just gone out of.

He'd promised to follow her, but he'd known her best chance of survival—since Jesse had been specifically targeting her when he'd walked in—was to get her the hell out and let him and hopefully Cam stop Jesse.

But a bullet had gone through the door Gracie was on the other side of.

Please God, let Gracie be okay.

Another gunshot went off, and if this one passed near him, he didn't feel it. Instead, something on the other side of the room crashed.

The lights suddenly flipped on, causing Will to wince and close his eyes on reflex. But he immediately forced himself to open them.

Cam was standing there, his own weapon drawn and pointed at Jesse. Will turned his attention to the large man in the middle of the room, his daughter cowering behind him.

Jesse smiled and Will didn't think, didn't hesitate. He got to his feet and ran full force at Jesse. He was more than shocked that a gunshot didn't go off before he crashed into Jesse's large, hard body.

He swore viciously as they both fell down, trying to reach out for the gun or land a blow with his non-broken arm. But it was all flailing limbs and painful landing on the hardwood floor.

Jesse swore and threatened, but he must have lost the gun because he was using both hands to try to toss Will off him. Will managed to land a blow to Jesse's gut with his knee, but the victory lasted only seconds before Jesse was twisting his broken arm.

Will fought to escape that painful grasp, fought to land any blow. He got a few in, but still Jesse twisted his broken arm until Will was shaking and sweating.

Will felt himself being nudged out of the way by a boot, but it got Jesse to let go of his arm so he could only feel relief flood him. Everything hurt and ached and Gracie...

Will stumbled to his feet and looked at Cam, who had his boot shoved into Jesse's neck and had his weapon pointed straight at him.

"You can't shoot me," Jesse growled, attempting to spit on Cam. He missed his mark and his eyes searched the room, but Kayleigh had taken off through the back, as if she could escape.

"Watch me." Cam flicked a glance at Will. "Go see if the cops are here yet."

Will was already scrambling for the door, aching arm forgotten. Screw the cops. Was Gracie okay?

He stumbled out the door, and there were two police cruisers. One had its lights on, the other was completely dark. Laurel stood talking to another deputy, while two other deputies stood on the porch, guns drawn on him.

"That's Cooper," Laurel shouted, striding forward. "What's the status?"

"Cam's got Jesse. Kayleigh went out the back."

"Mosely, Jackson, get Kayleigh Granger. Hart, go in and arrest Jesse Carson. Get statements from Cam and my father. I'll handle Will's."

The men moved at Laurel's orders.

"Where the hell is Gracie?"

Laurel dropped her crossed arms, running a hand through her hair that was falling out of its rubber band. It was the way her arm shook that had Will's stomach pitching.

Laurel cleared her throat. "She…"

"What?" Will demanded, and the only reason he didn't reach out and shake Laurel was that every inch of his body felt like lead. Painful, cracked lead.

"It was all his idea!" came a scream from the other

side of the house. "He threatened me! You have to let me go." The two deputies who'd gone after Kayleigh had her handcuffed and were bringing her toward one of the cruisers.

"Where is Gracie?" Will demanded when Laurel turned all her attention to Kayleigh.

"Will."

"Just tell me," he said, and he didn't have it in him to care that his voice broke.

"The bullet that went through the door hit her. I had the first deputy on the scene rush her to the hospital."

"She was…"

"Breathing? Yes. But it was not good."

"Why are we here? I have to go." He started walking. God knew where. He didn't have a car. Couldn't drive. But how could Laurel just let her be taken away to the hospital alone?

"Will, we have to handle this here." She caught up with him and gripped his good arm. "We cannot go running off to the hospital. I know you're scared. *I'm* scared, but we have to handle *this*."

"Like hell we do," he returned, pulling his arm out of her grip.

"Do you want Jesse Carson to go to jail?" she demanded.

Will stepped forward, furious she'd even question it—that she'd still be standing here when Gracie was being rushed to the hospital. After being shot. "He will rot there if I have anything to do with it."

"Then we have to do this right. We need statements and proof and they need to be arrested on the complete up-and-up. We wouldn't be with her in the hospital anyway. This is what we can do for her. This is what we *have* to do for her. Will. Us being in that hospital doesn't change anything. Us making sure this scum gets everything he has coming to him? That's something."

Will swallowed at the horrible tide of emotion rising in his throat. Somewhere in his brain he knew Laurel was right. Being with Gracie wouldn't change anything.

"How bad was it?"

"I don't know, Will. They're going to call me the second they have any information and we'll go to the hospital immediately once we get everything taken care of here."

Will nodded, looking back at the house where Jesse was being lead out the door. He struggled the whole way, trying to knock the deputies over, trying to land an elbow. But the deputies just kept pulling him toward one of the cruisers, Cam behind them, his gun still drawn.

Jesse looked around the yard, then at Will and Laurel standing. He struggled more in the handcuffs and the deputies' grips, but they didn't let him go.

"Where's the little bitch?" Jesse called. "Did I get her?"

Sucker shot or not, Will calmly walked over and punched Jesse right in the nose, satisfied by both the sickening crack and the howl of pain.

"Oops," Will said to both deputies who'd stopped pulling Jesse forward and were staring at him in shock.

"He assaulted me! I want to press charges!" Jesse screamed.

That got the deputies back into action and they struggled to get Jesse into the back of the car, Jesse fighting and yelling about Will and a broken nose the whole way.

"It doesn't solve anything," Laurel said softly. "But that was satisfying to watch."

"Laurel."

"Come on. We need your statement."

So he went with her, back toward the gigantic Delaney house now glittering with light. Enough light he could see the pool of blood on the porch. Gracie's blood.

He wished he'd done a lot more than break Jesse's nose.

Chapter Nineteen

You're too strong to give up.
   We're only getting started.
   All you have to do is open your eyes.
   I am *sorry.*
   Gracie couldn't make sense of any of the voices that came or went. They all existed in a gray fog. She couldn't isolate one from another, but they kept coming. Someone would take her hand, or whisper something to her, but she couldn't open her eyes. She couldn't even seem to breathe, though it wasn't a struggle exactly. She just didn't seem to have any control over anything.
   Grace. She hadn't heard that voice in so long and it sent a weird, twisted pain through her side. Her mother's voice. No one called her Grace nicely, lovingly. She hadn't been able to stand it after losing both parents, and only Uncle Geoff had refused to abide her wishes to go by Gracie. But he never said

Grace kindly, not like this. It had been almost twenty years since she'd heard that voice.

Grace. You'll be all right.

She remembered those words. Her mother's last. *You'll be all right.* She'd believed it. She'd always believed it because that had been Mom's parting gift to her.

When Gracie's eyes opened, it was as if someone had pulled her straight out of the fog. She hadn't made the choice to open anything, but suddenly her eyes were open and everything was a cloudy white.

Nothing made sense about any of this. Where was she? Why did she hurt? She didn't remember anything.

"Gracie."

Except she did remember that voice, and even though it took a supreme effort she didn't know she had in her, she turned her head toward it. Will's face was a little blurry, but it was Will. Right there. Oh, thank God. "I remember you," she whispered.

He made a noise she couldn't explain, but he leaned forward and pressed his forehead to the back of her hand. Because he'd been holding her hand.

"Well, that's something," he croaked. "Are there things you don't remember?"

His voice sounded so scratchy. So…something. But her head was pounding too much to really figure it all out. Her throat was dry and she felt so incredibly heavy.

"Hurts," she muttered even though that wasn't the right word for it. No throbbing pain or sharp discomfort. Just everything was too heavy, too hard.

"What does?"

"Everything."

"Oh, Gracie. Hell. I think you scared thirty years off all our lives. I'm supposed to go get everyone the second you wake up."

"No, don't go." She tried to hold on to him, but after the failed attempt she realized he hadn't made any move to go. Will. Here. Hers. But she didn't understand how she was in the hospital, and he wasn't. Wasn't he hurt? Jesse had hurt him. But after that? "It's all a jumble. What happened?"

"You were shot. Narrowly missed your spine. They say you were lucky."

"Shot." She squeezed her eyes shut trying to make sense of that. Of anything. Shot. Lucky. "Who shot me?"

"They've got you on a lot of medications. They said it'll take some time to come out of it. Make sense of things. It's okay if you're confused. It's all going to clear up."

"Will."

He kissed the palm of her hand, just a light brush of his lips. "That's me."

She managed to move her arm, reach up and touch the bandage on his head. "He knocked you out. Jesse. Jesse Carson. He hit you with something and knocked you out. You're okay. I didn't think you were okay."

Will gave her hand a light squeeze. "Lead pipe. Managed to get both me and Cam. But we're fine. A few stitches and a concussion for the both of us. I was given the extra-special warning that if I sustain another concussion my brain's probably mush, but I'm mostly okay. Sitting here instead of lying there, huh?"

"You pushed me out the door." It was fuzzy, but starting to come together. Jesse had taken her to her uncle's house and... Something she should remember. Something she should tell Will.

"I should have followed you out that door," Will said gravely, still holding on to her hand. "I should have done so many things differently. Like not listen to the psychopath in the first place. You'd be okay."

"No. I mean, first of all, I am okay, but he wanted me all along. It didn't really have anything to do with you. He wanted to punish my uncle." She tried to read through the fog. "I can't remember."

"You don't have to. Jesse is going to jail, and everyone else might be a little banged up here and there, but we're all going to live and that's what's important."

"But you blame yourself."

"I should have—"

"You can't tell me being alive is what's important and then tell me you should have done things differently. You can't sit there and blame yourself. The only blame for today goes on Jesse's shoulders."

"You're going to have this same guilt fight with Cam and Laurel, just to warn you."

She closed her eyes, unaccountably exhausted. "I don't want to fight. I want to go home."

"You're not quite ready for that, but waking up was a start."

"Mmm." She tried to open her eyes, but sleep seemed like a much cozier idea. Maybe in sleep she could find the answers.

"Gracie?"

"Hmm." But she was floating away, and whatever he said after that never quite reached her.

I LOVE YOU.

Will looked down at Gracie's pale face, gut twisted into knots over how much strength had leaked out of her in just thirty-six hours. She hadn't heard him say those three words, and maybe it was for the best. Probably shouldn't utter them in a hospital room to a gunshot victim.

The door opened and Laurel walked in, dressed in her uniform.

"She woke up for a second," he offered.

Laurel rushed over to the other side of the bed, peered down at Gracie. "Why didn't you come get us?" she hissed in a whisper.

"She didn't want me to leave."

"You could have used the nurse button."

"I didn't think of that at the time."

Laurel scowled at him. "What did she say?"

"She didn't remember everything. Still a little mixed-up, but she knew who everyone was and had a little idea of what happened. What's the update on Jesse?"

Laurel moved back to his side of the bed, then pulled him out of the chair and back toward the door. In a low voice, she spoke. "Charges include attempted murder, aggravated assault, coercion. I could go on, but even if he pleas down, he's going to be spending quite a bit of time in jail."

"What about Kayleigh?"

"She'll likely get off as she's given us almost all the information to prosecute Jesse to the fullest extent."

Will frowned. He didn't particularly like that Kayleigh wouldn't suffer any consequences, but maybe she really just was a pawn in her father's scheme.

"Now, visitor hours are over, and if you make the same scene you made yesterday about leaving, I will have to arrest you."

Will scowled. "Someone should be with her."

"Jen's in the waiting room. Since she's family, they're letting her spend the night." Laurel frowned, something like concern in her eyes. "They kept you overnight last night. Where are you going to stay tonight and how are you going to get there?"

Will glanced at Gracie, asleep in bed, an idea forming. He watched her as he lied to Laurel so the fib wouldn't show on his face. "Gracie said I could stay at her place. I just need a ride."

"I can do that. Should you be alone with that concussion?"

"It's been over twenty-four hours. They said I was fine to be alone after that." He turned to Laurel and smiled.

"Okay. Follow me."

"Just one second." He felt a little weird with Laurel watching him, but he couldn't just walk out. He went over to Gracie's bed and dropped a kiss to her temple, whispering a goodbye and those three idiotic words one more time.

He walked back to where Laurel was waiting by the door. She had a speculative look on her face and Will hunched his shoulders against it.

"What?"

"I didn't like you, Will. For two years, you've been nothing but a pain in my side and a constant worry because I knew Gracie had a thing for you and I thought you weren't interested. But you were right, and you've been... Well, I'm glad you're as head over heels for her as she is for you. Or I'd have to break some laws to cause you physical harm and probably lose my job."

"You could always have Grady do it and avoid the job loss."

"Smart. I'll keep that in mind."

"I wasn't not interested. I was clueless, and still healing I guess. So. It wasn't like that. Just so you know."

Laurel smiled, slinging her arm around his shoulders. "Now that I know, I can mock you mercilessly. I am marrying a Carson after all, and mocking is their way of life."

"I think I prefer the Delaneys."

"I think you're about to be dealing with a whole lot of both." She took a deep breath. "I've talked to my father."

"Ah."

"The affair didn't start before you guys moved here. There was no past connection. Do you remember Paula applying for finance officer?"

"Vaguely. She didn't get the job. That was only three or four years ago, right?"

"Right. She didn't get the job, but my father was the one who interviewed her." Laurel pulled a face. "He said they hit it off. They started meeting for drinks in Fairmont. Then, well, it escalated from there."

Will didn't know what to say. He supposed it was some kind of relief she hadn't been cheating on him the whole time. A relief he'd been wrong about *some* things.

"In addition to that, based on what Kayleigh told us, Jesse tampered with your car and burned down your house in the hopes you'd back off so he could arrange his revenge for my father."

"Why didn't he just kill Cam and I back at the bar?"

"He was trying to get my father in jail, not wind himself back there. Your saving grace, I guess."

Saving Grace. No, that was the woman in the hospital bed. The woman he was ready to build a future with. Because Paula, affairs and even this horrible incident was in the past.

It was time to plan his future.

GRACIE WASN'T SURE she'd ever been so happy to see her little house in her entire life. It seemed like months or years since this had all started even though it had been only two weeks now.

There was a dusting of snow over her Christmas lights lining the eaves, and thick clumps in the sparkling trees. The lights were on inside, adding another warm glow of welcome to the lights. No more white, sterile hospital. *Home.*

"Is someone inside?"

"Will," Laurel said, eyebrows drawing together. "He said you offered to let him stay at your house. I gave him your key."

"Oh. I don't remember. Maybe when I was out of it I did, but I'm glad I did. He doesn't have anywhere to go." She yawned and tried not to wince as Laurel helped her up the walk. The wound still hurt, and she imagined it would for quite a while, but she'd been lucky the bullet had passed through her side and not hit any important organs.

Her recovery had been stellar and now she was home just in time for Christmas tomorrow. And Will was inside. She smiled at that.

Laurel turned the knob and pushed the door open, helping Gracie with that last step. She was too exhausted to fight all the help she was getting, though she imagined she'd be done with it in a few days.

For today, she was glad to be home. Her Christmas tree twinkled from the corner and Will stepped out of the kitchen with a big grin on his face.

This was exactly what she wanted for Christmas. Maybe without the gunshot wound and his broken arm, but they'd get through those things all the same. Heal. Move on and forward.

"Welcome home," he offered with a smile.

Home. Will in her home. It felt infinitely, perfectly right. She stepped toward him and when she reached him she simply leaned right into him, gingerly to protect her side and his arm, but he wrapped his good arm around her and this was right where she wanted to be for a very long time.

"I guess I'll leave you two alone, huh?" Laurel smiled warmly. "Take care of each other, and for the love of God stay out of trouble."

"Merry Christmas, Laurel," Will offered.

"Merry Christmas, guys." She left, pulling the door closed behind her.

"Christmas," Gracie murmured, looking up at Will. "How did it get to be Christmas Eve?"

"I wish I knew." He used his good hand to brush some hair out of her face. "Oh, I'm glad you're here."

"Me, too," she replied emphatically.

"And I have a Christmas gift."

"But it isn't Christmas."

"It's our Christmas. You're home, which is my gift, and what I'd made for you survived my shop's destruction, so Christmas miracle or something."

"You made something for me before?"

"I did. I'd convinced myself I was going to sell it to the antique store while I made it, but it was always for you." He released her then bent under the tree and pulled a terribly wrapped lump that might contain a box somewhere under crumpled edges and too much paper. He cleared his throat. "It was hard to wrap with only one workable arm."

She swallowed, feeling teary as she carefully

pulled the wrapping paper away from the box inside. She pulled the lid open to find an iron door knocker in the shape of a flowering rose.

"You were always talking about how much you liked my door knocker. I'll install it for you, too, once I've got two good arms."

"Will. It looks just like the rose bushes I planted in front of your cabin."

"That was kind of the point." He smiled, and she realized a tear had escaped only when he reached out to brush it away.

She waved a hand in front of her face. "I'm blaming this emotional response on the meds."

"I don't mind an emotional response," he said, still touching her face.

The gift was thoughtful and gorgeous and proved Will had been paying attention even when he hadn't wanted to. It was too perfect, really. She didn't deserve it or him or this seemingly happy beginning.

Which reminded her of something she'd completely let fall into that fog that still clouded some of what had happened that night.

"Gracie, I lo—"

Oh God. No. "Wait."

"Huh?"

"Oh God. I haven't told you, all the things I pieced together. I didn't tell you." She turned away from him, panic bubbling through her. She hadn't told Will and it changed everything. *Everything.*

"Tell me what?" he insisted, moving so that he was in front of her again.

It was going to end things. How could it not? "I..." She didn't want to lose him, but how could she keep that secret? It was too big, too awful and likely to come out in Jesse's trial anyway. "Will, I know who Paula was having an affair with," she whispered.

He didn't say anything, just gave her a quizzical look.

"It was my uncle," she forced herself to say. "That's why Jesse was going to hurt me. That's what prompted Jesse to try to punish Paula—a relationship with a Delaney. I..." She shook her head, feeling tears well in her eyes as she looked down at his perfect gift.

She thrust it back at him. He wouldn't want her now. Not when she was connected to the man his wife had slept with.

"What are you doing?"

"You can't possibly want..." She forced herself to look at him and he only looked confused. Not shocked or angry or anything other than slightly concerned. "You don't want me now," she said firmly. "I'm related to the man who—"

"Gracie, I knew all that. Kayleigh told the police everything, and Laurel explained it all to me. Why

Jesse was there, how he was involved with killing Paula. I knew it was your uncle days ago." He took her by the shoulders, ignoring the gift she still held out to him. "I don't care who you're related to. I love you."

She could only stare at him for a few awful seconds. But he was still touching her. He knew and he'd given her this and said that. "But…"

"No buts. I love you no matter what. I'm not saying I want to have Christmas dinner with the guy, but that's also because he treats you like crap from what I can tell. But I love you, and I'll make sacrifices for you, Gracie. You've been there no matter how little I deserved it, and you infinitely deserve the same from me. Why would any of that stuff you had nothing to do with change my mind?"

No one had ever said that to her before. Not so certainly. Not without equivocations. But Will just *loved* her. No matter what.

"I love you, too," she whispered.

He grinned. "I kind of knew that."

Which earned him a laugh, but then she winced and placed a hand over her side. "Oh, don't make me do that for another few weeks."

"We should get you to bed," Will said, taking the present from her finally and putting it on the table next to the couch. "I'd carry you if I had two arms."

"Man, we really are a pair."

"A pair of survivors."

She smiled at that, walking with him down her hallway toward her bedroom. Survivors. Yes, they'd both survived a lot, and now they had each other to lean on to survive the rest.

And what could be a better Christmas gift than that?

* * * * *

COMING NEXT MONTH FROM

⊕ HARLEQUIN®

INTRIGUE

Available December 18, 2018

#1827 LAWMAN WITH A CAUSE
The Lawmen of McCall Canyon • by Delores Fossen
When a serial killer begins targeting the recipients of his late fiancée's organs, Sheriff Egan McCall must protect former hostage negotiator Jordan Gentry, the woman he blames for her death—and the one he can't stop thinking about.

#1828 SIX MINUTES TO MIDNIGHT
Mission: Six • by Elle James
Navy SEAL "T-Mac" Trace McGuire and his team are sent on a mission to find the source of a traitor selling arms to Somalian rebels. Tasked with protecting a sexy dog handler and her uniquely trained canine, T-Mac never planned on falling for the pretty soldier...

#1829 MISSING IN CONARD COUNTY
by Rachel Lee
When three girls go missing, only K-9 officer Kelly Noveno and her friend Al Carstairs continue searching after a violent winter storm buries evidence.

#1830 DELTA FORCE DIE HARD
Red, White and Built: Pumped Up • by Carol Ericson
Delta Force soldier Joe McVie secretly investigates a group of aid workers after they accuse his commander of planning an attack on a refugee camp. While he initially questions heiress Hailey Duvall, her own suspicion toward her companions ultimately puts her in danger. Now protecting her becomes the most important mission of Joe's career.

#1831 LAST STAND IN TEXAS
by Robin Perini
Desperate to protect her daughter, Faith Thomas flees her serial killer ex-husband. Now she is forced to rely on Léon Royce, a mysterious stranger with dangerous secrets of his own.

#1832 SHADOW POINT DEPUTY
Garrett Valor • by Julie Anne Lindsey
Can playboy deputy Cole Garrett win the tender heart of Rita Horn, a witness in his protection...or will his distraction prove deadly?

YOU CAN FIND MORE INFORMATION ON UPCOMING HARLEQUIN® TITLES, FREE EXCERPTS AND MORE AT WWW.HARLEQUIN.COM.

HICNM1218

SPECIAL EXCERPT FROM

HQN™

*When Ashley Jo "AJ" Somerfield is told that
Cyrus Cahill is missing and presumed dead,
she refuses to believe the worst. Now she will
do whatever it takes to bring him home.*

Read on for a sneak preview of
Wrangler's Rescue,
*the final book in The Montana Cahills series
by* New York Times *bestselling author B.J. Daniels.*

Ashley Jo "AJ" Somerfield couldn't help herself. She kept looking out the window of the Stagecoach Saloon hoping to see a familiar ranch pickup. Cyrus Cahill had promised to stop by as soon as he returned to Gilt Edge. He'd been gone less than a week after driving down to Denver to see about buying a bull for the ranch.

"I'll be back on Saturday," he'd said when he left. "Isn't that the day Billie Dee makes chicken and dumplings?"

He knew darned well it was. "Texas chicken and dumplings," AJ had corrected him, since everything Billie Dee cooked had a little of her Southern spice in it. "I know you can't resist her cookin' so I guess I'll see you then."

He'd laughed. Oh, how she loved that laugh. "Maybe you will if you just happen to be tending bar on Saturday."

"I will be." That was something else he knew darned well.

He'd let out a whistle. "Then I guess I'll see you then."

She smiled to herself at the memory. It had taken Cyrus a while to come out of his shell. One of those "aw shucks, ma'am" kind of cowboys, he was so darned shy she thought she was going to have to throw herself on the floor at his boots for him to notice her. But once he had opened up a little, they'd started talking, joking around, getting to know each other.

Before he'd left, they'd gone for a horseback ride through the snowy foothills up into the towering pines of the forest. It had been Cyrus's idea. They'd ridden up into one of the four mountain ranges that surrounded the town of Gilt Edge—and the Cahill Ranch.

It was when they'd stopped to admire the view from the mountaintop that overlooked the small western town that AJ had hoped Cyrus would kiss her. He sure looked as if he'd wanted to as they'd walked their horses to the edge of the overlook.

The sun warming them while the breeze whispered through the boughs of the snow-laden nearby pines, it was one of those priceless Montana January days between snowstorms. That was why Cyrus had said they should take advantage of the beautiful day before he left for Denver.

Standing on a bared-off spot on the edge of the mountain, he'd reached over and taken her hand in his. "Beautiful," he'd said. For a moment she thought he was talking about the view, but when she met his gaze she'd seen that he'd meant her.

Her heart had begun to pound. This was it. This was what she'd been hoping for. He drew her closer. Pushing back his Stetson, he bent toward her. His mouth was just a breath away from hers—when his mare nudged him with her nose.

She could laugh about it now. But if she hadn't grabbed Cyrus he would have fallen down the mountainside.

"She's just jealous," Cyrus had said of his horse as he'd rubbed the beast's neck after getting his footing under himself again.

But the moment had been lost. They'd saddled up and ridden back to Cahill Ranch.

AJ still wanted that kiss more than anything. Maybe today when Cyrus returned home. After all, it had been his idea to stop by the saloon his brother and sister owned when he got back. She thought it wasn't just Billie Dee's chicken and dumplings he was after, and bit her lower lip in anticipation.

Don't miss
Wrangler's Rescue *by B.J. Daniels,*
available December 2018 wherever
Harlequin® books and ebooks are sold.

www.Harlequin.com

Get 4 FREE REWARDS!

We'll send you 2 FREE Books plus 2 FREE Mystery Gifts.

Harlequin Intrigue® books feature heroes and heroines that confront and survive danger while finding themselves irresistibly drawn to one another.

FREE Value Over $20

SPECIAL EXCERPT FROM

⬡ HARLEQUIN®

I N T R I G U E

*When navy SEAL Trace "T-Mac" McGuire is tasked
with protecting a sexy dog handler, Kinsley Anderson,
and her uniquely trained dog, he never imagines
he will fall for her. As their search for a traitor selling
arms to Somalian rebels places them in increasingly
dangerous situations, can T-Mac keep
Kinsley—and his heart—safe?*

Read on for a sneak preview of
Six Minutes to Midnight
by New York Times *bestselling author Elle James.*

"Four days and a wake-up," Trace McGuire, T-Mac to
his friends, said as he sat across the table in the chow
hall on Camp Lemonnier. They'd returned from their
last mission in Niger with news they were scheduled to
redeploy back to the States.

He glanced around the table at his friends. When they
were deployed, they spent practically every waking hour
together. In the past, being stateside was about the same.
They'd go to work, train, get briefed, work out and then
go back to their apartments. Most of the time, they'd end
up at one of the team members' places to watch football,
cook out, or just lounge around and shoot the crap with
each other. They were like family and never seemed to
get tired of each other's company.

T-Mac suspected all that was about to change. All of
his closest SEAL buddies had women in their lives now.
All except him. Suddenly, going back to Virginia wasn't

quite as appealing as it had been in the past. T-Mac sighed and drank his lukewarm coffee.

"I can't wait to see Reese." Diesel tapped a finger against the rim of his coffee cup. "I promised to take her on a real date when I get back to civilization."

"What? You're not going to take her swinging through the jungle, communing with the gorillas?" Buck teased.

Petty Officer Dalton Samuel Landon, otherwise known as Diesel, shook his head. "Nope. Been there, done that. I think I'll take her to a restaurant where we don't have to forage for food. Then maybe we'll go out to a nightclub." He tipped his head to the side. "I wonder if she likes to dance."

"You mean you don't know?" Big Jake Schuler, the tallest man on the team, rolled his eyes. "I would have thought that in the time you two spent traipsing along the Congo River, you would know everything there was to know about each other."

Diesel frowned. "I know what's important. She's not fragile, she can climb a tree when she needs to, she doesn't fall apart when someone's shooting at her and she can kiss like nobody's business." Diesel shrugged. "In fact, I'm looking forward to learning more. She's amazing. How many female bodyguards do you know?"

Big Jake held up his hands in surrender. "You got me there. None."

Don't miss
Six Minutes to Midnight *by Elle James,*
available January 2019 wherever
Harlequin® *Intrigue books and ebooks are sold.*

www.Harlequin.com

Love Harlequin romance?

DISCOVER.

Be the first to find out about promotions, news and exclusive content!

Facebook.com/HarlequinBooks

Twitter.com/HarlequinBooks

Instagram.com/HarlequinBooks

Pinterest.com/HarlequinBooks

ReaderService.com

EXPLORE.

Sign up for the Harlequin e-newsletter and download a free book from any series at **TryHarlequin.com.**

CONNECT.

Join our Harlequin community to share your thoughts and connect with other romance readers!
Facebook.com/groups/HarlequinConnection

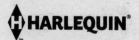

**ROMANCE WHEN
YOU NEED IT**

HSOCIAL2018